"What? Are you goin[g] asked, her tone scath[ing]

"Yeah, I would marry you.

Thought so. "But only because I'm pregnant! That's a crappy reason to be together, and we agreed! We agreed that this wasn't a long-term thing, that we'd use each other to have some fun, that it wasn't going to get serious!"

The anger died in Rowan's eyes, replaced by an icy intensity Jamie had never seen before. "Are you trying to tell me that you're not interested in trying to make a relationship work?"

She spread her fingers apart. "A baby complicates everything, Rowan! I don't want us getting sucked into this happy, everything-is-great, we're-going-to-be-parents false bliss and then realize that we have nothing more than sex and a baby in common!"

That was when she saw the flash of fire in his eyes...

Dear Reader,

Welcome to Annapolis, and let me introduce you to Rowan Cowper and Jamie Bacall, my oh-so-reluctant hero and heroine!

Jamie, a widow, is from a wealthy and connected East Coast family, and Rowan, a foster child turned self-made billionaire, is most definitely not. He stopped a fight, saved the life of a powerful man's son, and this action granted him access into the rarefied world of Maryland's elite.

Rowan and Jamie meet in an elevator and their scorching kiss leads to them sleeping together. But because their attraction makes them feel too much, they are both wary of taking their relationship any further. High passion can lead to catching feelings and that is something neither of these two commitment-phobes needs.

But as Jamie discovers, Rowan isn't that easy to dislodge, and before long, Jamie isn't sure whether that's what she wants! But how, after enduring the loss of her husband—an act she feels responsible for—is she supposed to trust love again? And will Rowan ever get the family he so badly needs and wants?

Happy reading!

With my very warm wishes,

Joss

Connect with me on:

Facebook: JossWoodAuthor
Twitter: JossWoodBooks
BookBub: joss-wood
Goodreads: Joss_Wood

JOSS WOOD

———

CROSSING TWO LITTLE LINES

Recycling programs for this product may not exist in your area.

ISBN-13: 978-1-335-58129-7

Crossing Two Little Lines

Copyright © 2022 by Joss Wood

For questions and comments about the quality of this book, please contact us at CustomerService@Harlequin.com.

Harlequin Enterprises ULC
22 Adelaide St. West, 40th Floor
Toronto, Ontario M5H 4E3, Canada
www.Harlequin.com

Printed in U.S.A.

Joss Wood loves books, coffee and traveling—especially to the wild places of southern Africa and, well, anywhere. She's a wife and a mom to two young adults. She's also a slave to two cats and a dog the size of a small cow. After a career in local economic development and business, Joss writes full-time from her home in KwaZulu-Natal, South Africa.

Books by Joss Wood

Harlequin Desire

Crossing Two Little Lines

Dynasties: DNA Dilemma

Secrets of a Bad Reputation
Wrong Brother, Right Kiss
Lost and Found Heir
The Secret Heir Returns

Harlequin Presents

South Africa's Scandalous Billionaires

How to Undo the Proud Billionaire
How to Win the Wild Billionaire
How to Tempt the Off-Limits Billionaire

Visit her Author Profile page at Harlequin.com, or josswoodbooks.com, for more titles.

You can also find Joss Wood on Facebook, along with other Harlequin Desire authors, at Facebook.com/harlequindesireauthors!

One

"Can you *please* stop breaking into my apartment?"

Jamie Bacall-Metcalfe shook her head at her brother, who was sitting at the small table in her kitchen, eyes on the screen of *her* tablet and drinking *her* coffee. Greg, just eleven months older than her, was dressed in shorts, sneakers and a less-than-fresh T-shirt, his dark hair wet with perspiration.

"I gave you a key for emergencies, not so you can use my place as a rest stop during your run," Jamie reminded him, keeping her tone mild. They both knew she was chastising him because she thought she should, not because she wanted him to stop dropping by. She adored her brother. He and his husband, Chas, were her best friends.

She nodded at his grungy T-shirt. "Can't you go home and shower and then break in?" Jamie asked, reaching for a coffee cup.

Greg patted the table, looking for his own coffee cup, his eyes still on the tablet. "Chas likes me nice and fresh. He's weird that way."

"So do I, actually," Jamie told him, walking over to peer over his shoulder. "What's caught your attention?"

Greg held up one finger, asking her to wait. Jamie sipped her coffee and allowed her eyes the supreme pleasure of looking at a headshot on the screen of a guy in his midthirties. Square jaw, straight nose, sexy mouth, brown hair with natural, streaky blond highlights. The right amount of stubble. But it was his eyes that caught and held her attention. They were an intense blue, the color of the wings on a blue morpho butterfly. Like the insect, all that intense blue was contained in a black ring. If he had a body to match the face, she could cast him in advertisements. Who was he, and how could she track him down? Sexy, masculine, handsome men who could look both sophisticated and sporty weren't easy to find.

Greg lowered the tablet to the table and leaned back in his chair, pushing his hand through the same dark brown hair they shared. Jamie took the seat next to him and nodded at the now-black screen. "So what's the news?"

And who was that guy? Jamie felt a frisson of attraction skitter up her spine, and it took her a few seconds to recognize it for what it was. Wow. So she wasn't a dried-up husk of a woman after all. Good to know.

"I was reading an article about Rowan Cowper."

Greg spoke as though she should know who Rowan Cowper was. She shrugged. "Who?"

Greg rolled his eyes. "Cowper Construction? He built the new hospital?"

"You are an architect and know builders, Gregory. I own an advertising agency, remember? I wouldn't mind putting Cowper in some of my ads, by the way."

"I wouldn't mind him putting his shoes under my bed," Greg commented.

"Your husband might object," Jamie said wryly.

"Chas is such a killjoy," Greg grumbled, and Jamie rolled her eyes. Her brother, being one of the most loyal men she knew, was all talk and no action.

"So why is he on the front page?" Jamie asked

Greg rose and refilled his coffee mug. "Ah…he was working late at one of his building sites and was heading back to his car when he came across a group of thugs mugging a college kid. It was three to one, and the kid was on the sidewalk, curled up, and they were kicking the crap out of him. Cowper arrived and proceeded to take down all three muggers solo… And the kid who was attacked is the governor's son. Cowper is being lauded as a hero."

Ah, now the picture was clear. Governor Carsten was a personal friend of her parents, who owned the very paper featuring Cowper. He had two children, the younger of whom had recently made a splash on social media when they came out as bisexual and nonbinary.

"Hate crime?" Jamie asked, feeling a little sick. Sometimes people sucked.

"The police aren't saying, but we know how often it happens. His father is the governor, the family is high profile, so it's not a stretch to believe he might've been targeted because of his family rather than his gender identity," Greg replied, wrapping his hands around his mug. "What isn't up for debate is that Cowper saved his life. The muggers had knives and were planning on using them."

Thank goodness he was there, Jamie thought.

Greg leaned back against the counter and looked at her, his expressive eyes narrowing. "Changing subjects—how are you doing, James Jessamy?"

Jamie scowled at him using her full name. What had her parents been thinking when they named her? Thank God they'd settled on calling her Jamie. "I'm fine, Gregory Michael Henry."

She knew what he was really asking. He had that worried-about-you look on his face. The fifth anniversary of her husband's death was coming up in a month, and it was her family's cue to check up on her more than usual.

She often wanted to tell them that the anniversary of Kaden's death wasn't particularly horrible. She thought about Kaden and relived the accident *every* day and felt as guilty now as she did five years ago. The guilt didn't come in waves; it was a constant presence. It was her fault the car had rolled, her fault he'd died.

"I'm fine, brother," she lied.

"No, you're not."

No, she wasn't. But she could pretend to be.

Rowan Cowper drained the whiskey in his glass and rolled his shoulders, wishing he could remove his tuxedo jacket and yank off his black tie. As his companion droned on, Rowan pulled back the sleeve of his jacket and took a discreet peek at his Patek Philippe Aquanaut, his most recent indulgence, and swallowed a sigh of relief. It was close to eleven, and soon he could leave this boring black-tie charity dinner that had been organized by the governor's wife.

He'd contributed a significant amount of cash but couldn't remember the cause. Children's cancer? The homeless? He should start paying attention or, better yet, stop coming to these stultifying events.

Option number two, please.

Rowan dropped out of the conversation and moved from the bar to the exit, making his excuses as people tried to talk to him. Not that long ago, he had been just another construction-company owner. Rich, sure, but not part of the highest echelons of Maryland society. Stopping a fight had resulted in an invitation to dinner at the governor's mansion and a sudden slew of invitations to the best society events in the state.

Not bad for a boy originally from West Gar-

field Park, Chicago, one of Illinois's most dangerous areas.

He wasn't a fool. He knew how the game was
played. Connections to the people who influenced
decisions were a smart business move and would
make his life easier.

A *lot* easier.

Rowan exited the ballroom, resisting the urge
to pull down his tie, and headed for the bank of
elevators on the far side of the entrance hall. His
time hadn't been wasted. He'd heard about land
about to be rezoned for commercial development
on the outskirts of the city and that a plastics plant
was building a new premises. He was interested in
both the land and the factory and had the names of
people to call.

Not a bad night's work. The downside, of course,
was having to duck the offers of dinner, drinks, a
night in bed. He'd refused them all.

Standing by the bank of elevators, he jabbed the
button with his finger and rubbed the back of his
neck, sighing when he heard a feminine voice calling his name.

Shona…something. They'd had a few dates, but
when she'd hinted he should meet her family, he'd
backed off. Way, way off.

He wasn't a meeting-the-family type of guy. The
only commitment he was capable of was to Cowper
Construction. It was his only love.

"Shona." Rowan winced when she rose up on her
toes to kiss one cheek, then the other.

Dropping her heels, she play-swatted his chest. "I'm so glad I ran into you! I haven't seen you for ages... Did you change your number? I've left you so many messages."

He was trying to think of a way to extricate himself without hurting her feelings when he felt an unfamiliar hand on his back. He whirled around and looked into the sparkling sherry-colored eyes of a brunette dressed in a slinky beaded silver dress. Her perfume, light and sexy, drifted up to his nose as she slipped her much smaller hand into his and leaned her temple against his shoulder.

His heart triple-thumped in his chest. Weird. It had never done that before.

"There you are! Sorry, I got caught up talking to Terry. He sends his best," she said, tipping her face up to look at him, smiling. It took him a couple of beats to remember that Terry was the governor.

God, with her flawless skin, big eyes and curvy body, she was heart-stoppingly beautiful.

She lifted one eyebrow in a challenge and turned her attention back to Shona, who now looked both bemused and belligerent. "Shona, are you well? How are your parents?"

Shona opened her mouth to speak, but Gorgeous Girl got there first. "Please send them my best wishes, but we must fly." She turned, slapped her hand on one of the closing doors to the elevator and tugged on Rowan's hand. "Babe, I've got a bottle of Moët on ice and whipped cream and strawberries in the fridge."

Strawberries and cream? Champagne? Yeah, he could easily imagine painting her skin with cream and licking it off. Dipping strawberries into champagne and sliding the plump fruit between those sexy lips?

Yes, please.

Rowan allowed her to pull him into the elevator. He looked back to see Shona standing there staring at them, her bottom lip wobbling. He was known for being a hard-ass, but he was still a sucker for a kick-me-when-I'm-down expression. He was about to speak when he felt Gorgeous Girl's grip on his hand tighten.

"Don't you dare. She's playing you," she muttered.

Right. Okay, then.

The elevator doors slid closed, and he pushed his free hand through his hair, feeling like he'd stepped through a portal into a strange new world.

Lovely, but weird.

What was she thinking, trying to rescue the very tall, very hot Rowan Cowper?

Did he even need rescuing? Maybe he wanted to take Shona back to his place and she'd just derailed his plans. Jamie shuffled from foot to foot, her hand still swallowed by his—so warm.

She looked up into those deep, intense eyes and bit the inside of her cheek. His face held no expression. She couldn't begin to imagine what was going on in his head, but she thought she caught the corners of his lips edging up, the start of a smile.

Well, at least he wasn't pissed.

She looked down at his hand holding hers. "You can let me go now."

He followed her gaze and immediately released her. "Sorry."

Her hand wanted to be back in his; it felt good there. "No need to apologize, I was the one who dragged you in here," Jamie replied. She pulled a face. "Did I read that situation wrong? Did you not need rescuing?"

Finally, that stern mouth morphed into a smile. "I've never needed rescuing, but thank you for trying."

She tipped her head to the side, hearing the truth in his words. He looked strong, powerful and incredibly capable. His eyes radiated a quiet intelligence that suggested there was no situation he couldn't get himself out of.

To be honest, now she felt foolish. She'd rushed in, thinking she was helping him but maybe she'd messed up. "Sorry if I spoiled your plans for this evening."

"You didn't. I was just heading home," he replied.

Right. That didn't tell her anything. What was it about this man that made her feel jittery? She met good-looking men all the time—both at work and at these social events she occasionally attended—but none of them made her feel warm in places that hadn't felt heat in a long while.

She recognized him earlier, immediately remembering him from the article Greg pointed out six weeks ago. He was even better looking in real life, and because she hadn't been able to keep her eyes from straying in his direction she'd noticed the slight shifts in his demeanor, from attentive to resigned to bored. And that was why she'd noticed he looked uncomfortable talking to Shona.

He made her think too much, see too much, feel too much. Suddenly, Jamie wanted to step out of the elevator, desperate to put some distance between her and the inscrutable Rowan Cowper. She was comfortable in her numb cocoon woven by guilt and grief. After what happened with Kaden, it was safer for her to stay distant, to not engage.

And yet she met Rowan's eyes instead.

Zzzztzzzt...zap.

She'd heard of sparks flying, but this was the first time it had happened to her. There was a force within her, urging her to wind her arms around his strong, tanned neck and taste his mouth. She couldn't go one more second without knowing whether he tasted as dark and dangerous as she suspected...

His eyes dropped to her mouth. She felt—rather than heard—his sigh, saw his eyes deepen to an inky blue and held her breath as he leaned down to...touch the console behind her.

"I presume you are heading for the lobby?" Rowan asked politely.

Well, damn. She'd been imagining a hot kiss and he couldn't wait to get away from her.

Way to go, Jamie. Your imagination is on fire tonight.

"Basement garage, actually," she replied, cursing the heat in her cheeks. Rowan stared at the console, his brows pulling down into a frown. "That's weird."

"What?"

"We're going up, not down. And the numbers are jumping out of order." The car dropped a floor, then shuddered, stopped and started heading up again. Rowan punched the button for an upcoming floor. "We need to get this thing to stop and catch another elevator."

"Okay," Jamie agreed.

The elevator started heading down again.

"Eight, seven, six, five…" Jamie counted down the floors and waited for the elevator to stop and let them out. It shuddered again, sighed and then stopped.

"Shit," Rowan muttered. "That's not good."

He turned to look at her and shrugged. "We might be here for a while. If ours is stuck, then they may all have problems. It might take them a while to get to us."

Fabulous.

Two

Rowan finished his call, looked down at his smartphone and grimaced. His eyes connected with Gorgeous Girl's as he pushed his phone into his pants pocket. "It's as I thought—all the elevators are malfunctioning. They are going to get the older people and kids out first, so we'll be the last to be rescued, I'm afraid."

To his surprise, she just shrugged before bending and lifting her right foot. "If I'm going to be stuck here for a while, then these instruments of torture are coming off."

He didn't blame her. Rowan shrugged out of his jacket, pulled down his tie and released the top button of his shirt. Feeling like he could breathe, he turned his jacket inside out and placed it on the floor. "I don't think it's a good idea to get that dress dirty. It looks like hell to wash, so sit on my jacket."

She sent him a grateful look, her hand skimming over her beaded bodice. "Thank you. And, yes, it is a pain to wash, but it's worth it. I shouldn't be wearing it, but every couple of years I pull it out, fall in love again and can't resist slipping it on," she told him as she sat down, her back against the wall of the elevator and her legs stretched out. She had a tiny bumblebee tattoo on the inside of her ankle, and her toenails were painted shell pink.

Rowan dropped down to sit next to her, keeping a decent nonthreatening distance between them.

He looked into those fabulous eyes and realized that he couldn't call her Gorgeous Girl for the rest of the evening. "I didn't catch your name."

"I'm Jamie Bacall-Metcalfe."

Jamie…it suited her. He looked down at her dress, puzzled. "Sorry, I'm trying   and failing— to work out why you shouldn't wear the dress. Did you steal it? Borrow it without asking?"

He was surprised at the words flowing from his mouth; he rarely spoke so much, and never to a stranger. Then again, most people were strangers.

Her laugh was surprisingly deep and very sexy. "No, I didn't steal or borrow it," she replied, smoothing the fabric over her slim thighs. "It's a rare dress from the twenties, so it's over a hundred years old."

He turned his head to stare at her. The dress looked like it had been made yesterday. "Really?"

She nodded, then sighed. "I'm a sucker for old

clothes, vintage jewelry, the twenties and thirties. I knocked over a glass of red wine, and I narrowly missed having it land on me. So I thought it was time to leave."

He saw something flicker in her eyes, and he knew she spoke the truth—just not the whole truth. "What else happened tonight?"

Those amazing eyes widened, then narrowed. "How on earth do you know something happened?"

He could tell her that six years spent in some rough foster homes had made him a master of reading body language. His ability to see the smallest change in someone's eyes, shoulders or lift of the lips had saved his skin on more than a few occasions. But he didn't explain. Nobody knew of his past and never would.

He watched her turn a solid gold band around and around the ring finger of her right hand. Her left hand—thank God—was bare. He didn't want her to have a husband, fiancé or significant other waiting for her at home.

Why? God only knew.

"What else happened tonight?" he repeated his earlier question.

She dropped her hands into her lap and rested the back of her head against the wall. She turned to look at him and grimaced. "I was with my parents and grandmother, and a guy sitting at our table invited me to have dinner with him. I tried to get out of it gracefully, but my family was pushing me to accept. So I knocked over a glass of red wine so I could leave."

She sighed. "I keep telling my family that I'm fine on my own, but they believe I need to get back on the horse."

She'd lost him. What horse? "Sorry?"

She looked down at her hands. "I haven't dated for a long time, and they want me to." She released an annoyed sigh. "And that's only partly true. They want me to date, then marry, then produce a child, because I'm the only hope for carrying on the family line."

He winced. He'd never experienced family pressure, but it didn't sound like fun. "Is passing on the family genes so important? Do you have a rare genetic advantage the world needs?"

She laughed at his teasing, and he felt his throat tighten, his stomach warm. When was the last time he had made a woman laugh? Years ago? Never?

"None of the above, sadly. Have you heard of the Bacalls?"

Of course. Everyone who lived in Annapolis knew of the family. The Bacalls owned a media empire and had interests in tech. Old money, they were the bluest of Maryland blue bloods.

"Sure, I've heard of the family—but when you say 'Bacall,' my mind immediately goes to Greg Bacall. He's an incredible architect who specializes in designing green buildings."

Pleasure lit up her eyes. "Greg is my brother. I'll admit he is brilliant, but he's also a pain in my ass."

He heard the affection in her voice and felt a little envious. He would've loved a brother or sister. More than that, he would've loved a parent who cared about him enough to keep him around. But he was over wishing for a family, for things that wouldn't come true.

People had a habit of leaving him. He was destined to live his life solo. That was a truth he'd accepted a long time ago.

"Can't your brother help out with the continuation of the family line?" he asked, fascinated by her family dynamics.

"Greg is gay, and while he and Chas could have kids—surrogacy, adoption, whatever—they don't want any. So I'm my mother's and grandmother's last hope. They are both obsessed with the idea of a baby to coo over," she said.

He couldn't help the next question. His curiosity was burning a hole in his head. "Two questions… Why isn't there a Mr. Jamie at home? And do you want kids?"

He caught a distraught flicker in her eyes, saw her jaw tense. "It's a long story and, no, I don't want kids either."

Oh, now that was a lie. He cocked his head to the side. "Really?"

She nodded. "Oh, yeah. Not interested." But when she refused to meet his eyes and glanced at the elevator door instead, as if looking for an out, his suspicion that she was fudging the truth was confirmed.

But because he hated people digging into his own psyche, he decided not to pursue the topic. Her body, her life. Her mother's and grandmother's disappointment.

"God, I'm hungry," Jamie said after a long sigh. As if to emphasize, her stomach rumbled.

Rowan grinned when she blushed.

Jamie bent her legs and rested her forearms on her knees. "Distract me, Cowper."

Her eyes connected with his, and he felt the pull, saw the hot flare of desire in her eyes, the way her breath caught and her shoulders tensed. He couldn't ignore the flush on her cheeks and the throbbing pulse point in her neck. And another good clue—underneath those tiny beads on the bodice of her dress, her nipples were tight and erect. She was as attracted to him as he was her.

He could dip his head, hold her face, kiss her senseless. And, God, he wanted to. He was very sure she wouldn't object. If they reacted to each other the way he thought they might—with bone-melting intensity—they'd probably take this too far.

And that wasn't wise. Not in an elevator...

So he hunted around for a neutral topic. "How do you know me?" The answer came to him before she could answer. "That damn newspaper article," he muttered.

"Yep." Jamie nodded. "I've been coming to these social events since I was a teenager, and I've never seen you around before. I take it your newfound popularity is due to the governor's gratitude?"

Bluntly put but true. "Accurate."

"And you're here because making friends with the power brokers might help your business."

A frown pulled her dark eyebrows together as she glanced at his watch. He knew she was curious as to how much help he needed if he could afford one of the most expensive watches in the world.

He wondered if she'd understand that it wasn't a matter of money. Having grown up in this world, would she understand that being invited to these events was the equivalent of being asked to join an exclusive club? To someone like him, someone who hadn't been born with a silver spoon in his mouth, these types of invitations had been nonexistent before his chance encounter with the governor's son.

Bigger and better construction deals, the ones with prestige, had also been out of his reach.

"Sometimes it's not *what* you know but *who* you know," he told her. "I work hard and I work smart, but sometimes that's not enough." He wouldn't say more. He'd run his mouth too much already.

"I get that. My dad gets so frustrated with the great and the good of Annapolis. He says the snobs cut off their noses to spite their faces, because they deal with the same incompetent, inefficient, lazy people just because they went to boarding school or played polo together."

"I think I'd like your dad."

"You probably would," Jamie admitted. "Despite being the fifth generation to run Bacall Media, he's the most chill, low-key, unsnobby guy you'll ever meet. My mother is equally down-to-earth but my grandmother…" Jamie threw up her hands in despair. "Well, to put it mildly, she thinks she's Annapolis's answer to the Dowager Countess Crawley."

"Who?"

"You haven't watched *Downton Abbey*," she accused him.

He had the urge to apologize. "I don't watch TV."

"Never?"

"I catch a game now and then. The news."

"How do you relax, wind down?" she demanded.

He didn't. "I exercise, sometimes read." Though he couldn't remember the last book he'd read for fun. Or when. "I mostly work."

Her expression suggested that work made Rowan a very dull boy. She wasn't wrong. Needing to change the subject again, he asked, "Do you enjoy these types of events?"

She wrinkled her nose. "Not really. I'm expected to show my face. Not to be boastful, but my family is influential, and I am what they call 'a catch.' Powerful family, lots of money, reasonably good-looking."

If *reasonably good-looking* was a euphemism for *freaking gorgeous*, then okay.

"But I'm not naive, and I know most of the men who ask me out are more interested in the family fortune and connections than they are in me."

He thought she was underestimating her appeal but he knew where she was coming from. He never knew whether he was being hit on because he was wealthy and fresh on the market or because his face had been plastered across the front page.

Nobody really knew him. Mostly because he never let himself be known. He kept people at a distance and, if pushed, he'd admit to being emotionally stunted. Could he be blamed for being that way?

Throughout his life, every time he made a personal connection—whether it was with a social worker, a teacher, a friend or a foster parent—that person had been ripped from him in one way or another.

He protected his emotional core and never indulged in personal conversations...until now. With Jamie.

But only because they were stuck in an elevator, and not talking would be weird. He was reticent and uncommunicative but not weird. He hoped.

"I wish I could hang up an 'I'm off the market' sign. I just want to be alone. I'm not interested in dating or a relationship or being one-half of a couple."

Wow. That was quite a statement. And since every word she'd uttered was coated with sincerity, he believed her. This wasn't a woman playing hard to get. This was a woman who wanted her freedom and her solitude.

Jamie nudged his side with her elbow. "I bet you get hit on all the time too. Here? Tonight?"

He wasn't the type to boast, so he just shrugged.

Jamie grinned and nudged him again. "You so did!"

He didn't kiss and tell.

After a surprisingly comfortable silence, Jamie spoke again, her tone wry. "Here we are, sitting in an elevator after spending far too much money on a ticket to a charity fundraiser. We've drunk expensive booze, eaten expensive food—"

"Not a lot of it," Rowan corrected.

She nodded. "Not a lot of food but expensive,

nonetheless. And now we're complaining about the fact that people want to date us. I think we are whining, because those are such first-world, one-percent, rich-people problems."

Yeah, they were. But he'd come from poverty, knew what it was like to have nothing, to not eat for a day or two, to struggle to make a rent payment. "I hear you, but being rich doesn't insulate you from loneliness, from problems, from feelings and, in your case, from interfering relatives."

Their eyes connected, and Rowan watched as hers darkened with desire. His heart sped up when her mouth curved into a small genuine smile. "That's pretty deep, Cowper."

"I'm a pretty deep guy."

"Are you?" she whispered, her eyes moving from his mouth to his eyes and back again.

"Yeah. I'm also a guy who wants to kiss you."

Jamie half turned to face him and hooked her arm around his neck, pulling him closer. "Kiss away."

Rowan didn't hesitate. He covered her mouth with his, learning its shape, testing the softness. He placed his hand on the side of her face, tipping her head to the angle he preferred as he nibbled her full bottom lip and stroked his thumb over her high cheekbone. Needing to taste her, he probed the seam of her mouth with his tongue, and she opened, allowing him to slide inside. She tasted of wine and wonder.

They spent a few minutes exchanging long, lazy kisses, her fingers in his hair, his one hand on her back. But further exploration was hampered by their position. He needed her breasts pushing into his chest, his cock against her stomach. Without thinking, he wrapped his arm around her waist and hauled her onto his lap so that she sat sideways across his thighs. A loud rip of fabric made them jerk back to stare at each other.

"Shit! Was that your dress?" Rowan demanded, his heart sinking.

Jamie looked down and gasped when she saw a six-inch gap revealing the curve of her breast. "Oh, dear."

Oh, dear? He'd damaged her hundred-year-old dress and that was her reaction? "God, I'm so sorry."

She shrugged, seemingly unconcerned. "It tore at the seam. I'm sure it can be repaired." She placed her hand on his cheek, her thumb swiping over his bottom lip. "Now, where were we? Here, I think," Jamie said, lowering her mouth to his.

His head spinning, he leaned into her to take everything she was offering. He fell into her scent, her taste, reveling in the feel of her slim body in his arms, her hip pushing into his cock. Delicate, sexy, feminine as hell. His hand curled around her breast, and he sighed when she arched her back to push into his palm.

Yeah, she wanted him. The thought made his head spin.

Rowan brushed his thumb across her nipple, lost in the moment, in her mouth.

"Folks, we have a team on their way to you, and

they'll be pulling you out soon. Thank you for your patience."

Rowan stiffened at the sound of the strange voice floating through the elevator's speakers and winced when he remembered that most elevators these days had cameras that livestreamed video into a manned security room. They'd given someone quite a show.

Rowan banged his head against the back wall and muttered a hopefully indistinguishable curse. He patted Jamie's hip and gently lifted her off him before bounding to his feet. Holding out his hand, he took hers and pulled her to her feet. Standing, he saw the rip in her dress was worse than he'd thought. She was about to give their rescuers a very nice view of her right breast.

He winced. "God, I'm so sorry about your dress. That's far worse than red wine."

She looked down and grimaced. "Good thing I know a really good tailor."

"I'll pay to have it fixed," Rowan offered, bending down to pick up his jacket. Digging inside the pockets, he removed his slim wallet containing his credit cards and his car fob. Jamming both into his pants pocket, he flung his jacket around Jamie's shoulders.

"Put this on."

Jamie pushed her arms into the sleeves, and his jacket covered her to midthigh. She flapped her arms, and the ends of his jacket jumped up and down. He rolled up the fabric of one arm until her wrist was exposed. Then he started on the other arm. When he was done, he buttoned the jacket lapels together.

Jamie looked up at him, amused. "You're very good at taking charge and getting things done."

He supposed he was. *When there is nobody to look after you, you get on and look after yourself. And then you look after the people younger and smaller than you.* It was what he knew, how he lived his life.

"Folks, we're coming in," a voice said from outside the elevator doors.

Rowan picked up Jamie's shoes and bag before pulling her away from the door. He bent his head to speak in her ear. "This is the most fun I've had in an elevator—ever."

Jamie flashed him a brilliant smile. "Me too." She placed her hand on his arm and squeezed. "Thanks for not making this weird by asking me out on a date or asking if you can see me again."

He'd been about to do exactly that... *Shit.* "We did kiss," he pointed out. "And it's obvious there's chemistry."

She shrugged. "Yeah, there is and the kiss was fantastic but..."

His heart dropped to his toes. "Not interested?"

She shook her head. "Interested? Sure. Ready? No."

He heard the sadness in her voice and wondered what put the devastation in her eyes. "Will you ever be ready?" he asked. Though why he was asking, he had no clue. It wasn't like he wanted a relationship—with her or anyone.

"Probably not," Jamie replied. She squeezed his

arm again and reached up to kiss the corner of his mouth. She'd no sooner dropped back down to her toes than the elevator doors opened, and Rowan saw the smiling faces of their rescuers. Their elevator car was at least two feet down from the hallway passage.

The younger of the two responders grinned at Jamie and held out his hands. "If you give me your hands, I can pull you up."

"I've got her," Rowan brusquely told him. Standing behind Jamie, he gripped her hips and easily lifted her so that her feet rested on the ledge. A small push on her butt and she was in the hallway. He handed up her bag and shoes and hoisted himself up onto the ledge.

"Thanks, guys," she told the responders.

Rowan held her elbow as she put her shoes back on, then escorted her to the door leading to the stairs, where a line of people stood, slowly edging their way through.

"Hey, my folks must've gotten stuck in another elevator," Jamie exclaimed, gesturing to a tall, distinguished man and his pretty wife, who looked a lot like Jamie. "I'll walk down with them."

Their time together was over. Rowan briefly clasped her hand. "If I ever get stuck in an elevator again, I hope it's with you."

She flashed him another blinding smile and nodded. "It was nice being stuck with you, Cowper."

Then she, and his jacket, walked out of his life.

Three

Two weeks later, Jamie walked into the reception area of Cowper Construction—pretty, swish offices in a multistory high-rise in downtown Annapolis—and looked around at the sleek couches and bold art on the walls. A buff guy stood behind a granite counter, a headset over his shaved head. He held up his finger, asking her to wait. Jamie nodded and walked over to the wide window looking down at the busy city street below.

She draped Rowan's jacket, recently laundered, over the closest chair and looked at her watch. It was ten before six, and she knew she shouldn't be here. She had a pile of work sitting on her desk, and her parents expected her for dinner tonight.

Her family seemed to need to constantly take

her emotional temperature. Was she lonely? Was she coping?

She was a widow, someone who'd loved her husband, despite their issues. Yes, she still felt guilty; she always would. But she wasn't miserable. Unfortunately, it seemed her mom and grandmother would only accept that she was fine—whatever that meant—when she was in another relationship.

Not going to happen.

They would be thrilled to know she'd kissed Rowan—such a weak description!—and part of her was tempted to tell them. But a bigger part of her wanted to keep their kiss to herself. It was amazing and precious and unexpected and...

Well, lovely.

Everything about being in his arms had been sensational, from the heat rolling off him to the heady combination of his cologne and masculine scent; from the hardness of his thighs to his spice-and-sex mouth. She could've kissed him for millennia, lost in a world created just for the two of them. One filled with bright colors, intense sensations...heat.

The loud jangle of the receptionist's phone pulled Jamie back to the present, and she shook her head. What had she been about to do? Oh, right. She was going to text her mom.

Won't make it tonight. Sorry. Xxx

Her return message landed ten seconds later.

I expect you here by eight. Not one minute later. Love you!

Blergh. Her mother was persistent.

Jamie scrolled through her messages and saw a couple of invitations to upcoming events. She sighed. Her folks would be disappointed if she didn't attend the Gordons' private beach picnic— a catered affair for a hundred people—and the Jacksons' thirtieth wedding-anniversary party. The Bacalls, Gordons and Jacksons had a friendship that went back generations. She'd attended the same schools as their kids.

Her presence would be expected, and if she went to either function solo, as she usually did, there would be the same old clucking behind her back: "Poor Jamie. She still hasn't recovered, you know. She hasn't had a relationship since Kaden died…"

And she doubted she ever would.

Jamie placed her hand on the window, easily conjuring up Kaden's face, his green eyes, the red-gold stubble on his cheeks and chin. His mouth had been quick to smile, and she'd hoped their kids would inherit his dark red hair.

Their kids… The kids they'd never have.

Their inability to conceive had been the subject of the argument they'd had as they'd made their way to what was supposed to have been a sexy weekend away. Jamie couldn't remember how the fight started, but she did remember shouting at him to stop harping on the subject. He'd yelled back and taken his eyes off the road for too long. He'd missed the corner, skidding on the icy road.

She very much remembered hearing the car ripping apart, the screech of metal, the smell of blood, looking at Kaden's face when the world stopped spinning. For as long as she lived, the labored sound of his breathing would haunt her nightmares. Then the light in his eyes dimmed and he slipped away…

"Jamie?"

She whipped around, hand on her heart, to see Rowan standing a few feet from her, looking puzzled. Guilt, sorrow and sadness faded as she took in his big body, his quizzical expression. How was it that he could pull her into the present, grounding her in the here and now?

"Hi." The small word was all she could manage.

"Hi," he replied, frowning. "I called your name, but you were zoned out."

Jamie worried her bottom lip between her teeth. Whenever she went down that wormhole of memories, she zoned out, sliding into the memories of those horrible hours on that lonely road—praying, crying, screaming for help, begging for forgiveness.

"Sorry," Jamie said, pulling up a smile. She looked around, saw that the reception area was now empty and that the lights had been dimmed. "Wow, this place clears out fast."

"You've been standing for a while, ten minutes or so," Rowan told her.

That long? Dammit. She'd lost time before but never for so long and not in someone else's space.

"I'm so sorry. It's busy at work, and I have a lot on my mind."

He raised his eyebrows, his expression telling her that he didn't believe her off-the-cuff explanation. Rowan was dressed in chino pants and a navy button-down shirt, his sleeves rolled up. His brown leather belt matched his shoes, and he looked as good as he did in a tuxedo. Frankly, Cowper could wear a brown paper bag and still look hot. If she ever got to see him naked, she might spontaneously combust.

"It's nice to see you, but why are you here?"

Jamie quickly gathered her thoughts. There was a reason she was here, right? What was it? Her eyes fell on the packet containing his dry-cleaning, and she gestured toward it. "I brought your jacket back. I had it dry-cleaned."

"Thank you," Rowan replied. "I appreciate that. Oh, did you manage to get your dress fixed? I said I'd pay for the repairs."

She winced and shook her head. "I didn't, unfortunately. My tailor said the fabric ripped in a bad place and can't be repaired."

"I am so sorry. I know how much you love that dress."

She shrugged. "It was my fault for wearing it." Jamie placed her hands behind her back, her palms resting on the glass behind her. She looked around. "I like your offices. Very smart."

"What were you expecting?" Rowan asked, smiling. "A double-wide with battered desks on a construction site?"

Well, sort of. Okay, yes—not that she'd admit that to him. She nodded toward a corner office with glass walls. "Is that yours?"

"Mmm-hmm. Since you're here, would you like a drink?" Rowan asked.

She very much would. She should be sensible, hand his jacket over and leave. But she didn't want to. She wanted to have that drink, look at him some more and, yes, kiss him again. Maybe even do more than that. She knew she was playing with fire, but she'd step back before she got burned.

Her heart was encased in steel and ice. It was impenetrable. She could handle a mild flirtation, maybe even a one-night stand, with the very sexy Rowan Cowper. She'd walked through hell. A few flames didn't scare her.

Jamie picked up his dry-cleaning with one hand and hoisted her bag up onto her shoulder with the other.

"Sure."

Jamie followed Rowan across the reception area to his glass-walled office.

He hadn't been in his office earlier, or she would've noticed him sitting behind his wide, messy desk, the incredible view of downtown Annapolis to his right. At the open door, Rowan stepped back and gestured her inside his sanctum. There was a low couch situated against the wall and a small boardroom table tucked into another corner. But his view of the city dominated the space, and Jamie headed over to the L-shaped bank of floor-to-ceiling windows, enchanted. Dusk was falling and the city was starting to light up. What a magical time of day.

"Your view is amazing, Rowan," she said, her voice husky.

"My view *is* pretty spectacular."

Something in his voice made her turn, and she immediately noticed he wasn't looking at the buildings or the harbor but at her. Their eyes connected. He smiled and moved his gaze across her face, taking in her hair pulled into a high ponytail, the bold necklace she wore around her neck. He skimmed over her white silk top tucked into no-nonsense wide-legged black pants. His lips kicked up at the corners when he caught sight of her red-painted toes. He spent a moment looking at them, and she felt a low throb deep in her womb.

Feeling jittery from his intense look, she yanked her eyes off him and looked around his office. The glass walls had turned dark, and she could no longer see into the reception area.

"Is there a reason you've switched the walls from clear to opaque?" Jamie asked him, her heart rate climbing fast. She wasn't scared to be alone with him—not in the least. If anything, she was scared he *wouldn't* kiss her or touch her.

And maybe that was why she was here.

She wanted to be in his arms, to feel her mouth under his, to lightly rake her nails across the skin of his back, his butt. He was the first person in five years to make her feel alive, like a woman who had wants and needs.

"There are still people working late, and I thought we needed some privacy."

"For what?" she asked.

He quickly crossed the space between them, standing so close she felt the heat radiating off him, inhaled his cologne, brushed her shirt against his. He bent his head, his mouth a whisper from hers. "This. Let me kiss you again, Jamie."

Of course she would; wasn't that why she was here? To experience the magic of being in his arms again?

"I thought you'd never ask," Jamie whispered, moving her body closer to his.

She caught his smile before his mouth covered hers with devastating accuracy. He didn't hesitate, and his confidence was sexy as hell. Jamie grabbed his shirt and twisted it around her fist, using her grip to keep herself steady as he decimated her self-control.

She wanted this man—more than she'd ever wanted anyone, ever. She wanted him naked, on the couch or the floor or the desk, while the lights of Annapolis bathed their bodies.

This was unexpected and scary. What was it about this man, this stranger, that made her act so out of character? She didn't do one-night stands, never had. When she chose a lover, she did so with deliberation and after some time second-guessing herself.

And those choices had only happened in the years before she'd met and married Kaden, when she was young and far more impetuous than she was now.

But she couldn't walk away from Rowan. Not until she knew what it felt like to make love to him.

Even if it was in his office on a Tuesday evening in July.

Rowan wrapped her hair around his fist, gently pulling her head back to look up at his face. "I want to see you naked."

He was so very honest, so damn forthright. She liked that about him; she knew where she stood. She loosened her grip on his shirt and ran her hand over his rib cage, down his hip. "I've been imagining you naked too."

His eyebrows raised. "You've been thinking of me?"

Yes, far too much. "Only in an X-rated nighttime-fantasy type of way," she clarified.

He kissed her nose, then the corner of her mouth. "Good to know. I've been thinking of you too. In a double-X all-day-fantasy type of way."

Her inner romantic sighed, but her pragmatic side immediately reminded her that this was about sex, nothing more. She touched his cheek with the tips of her fingers, loving the feel of his stubble.

"Want to go somewhere?" she asked.

"If we do, will I get to see you naked?"

She thought about hedging, playing it coy, and brushed off the urge to play games. He was a blunt guy; she could be blunt too. "There's a damn good chance."

Rowan flashed that rare pirate grin that made her skin goose bump with pleasure. "Excellent," he said, grabbing her bag with one hand and her hand with the other. Tugging her to the corner of his office, he opened a floor-to-ceiling door concealing an elevator. Rowan pushed her inside, stepped into the small space after her and hit the only button on the panel. They immediately started flying up.

Twenty seconds later the elevator door opened, and Rowan walked backward, pulling her into his spacious penthouse apartment. She looked around, her jaw dropping at the double-volume bank of windows that offered even more sweeping views of the city's skyline and the harbor. Her quick visual sweep of the apartment told her it was dotted with the occasional piece of high-end Italian furniture, that she was standing on hardwood floors and that his kitchen was small but state-of-the-art.

Rowan clutched her hand and pulled her down a hallway, passing one bedroom, then two more, before pulling her inside a corner room dominated by a massive bed. Doors led onto his private patio and what looked to be a hot tub.

She could just imagine sitting there on a warm summer evening— or in the snow—kicking back and taking in the view.

Rowan gently gripped her jaw and forced her to look at him. "You with me?"

Was she? Did she want this?

Yes. Yes, she did.

She didn't *want* to want it, which was a totally different thing. Over the years, Greg and Chas had urged her to get her head, and body, back in the game. They'd told her, repeatedly, that she was too young to hide away, to sacrifice herself on the altar of regret and grief. Up until that Saturday night, she hadn't had the energy or the interest, but Rowan stirred her comatose libido to life. Now, it was demanding she engage.

And that was why she'd made the trek across town to his offices, why she'd used the return of his jacket as an excuse to see him. Because he made her feel alive, more *Jamie*, than she'd felt for years and years. With him, her guilt was sidelined, subdued.

He didn't expect anything more from her than this moment, wasn't asking for anything but for her to share her body with him. There was such freedom in living in the moment and not worrying about tomorrow, or next week, or next year.

"Your apartment is huge."

"I'll give you the tour later," he promised. "Right now, I want to explore you."

His words should've sounded cheesy, like a smoothly delivered line, but she saw the sincerity and admiration in his gaze and slowly nodded. She closed her eyes, hauled in a deep breath and felt his hands drop away.

When Jamie looked at him again, she saw that he'd put a healthy amount of distance between them, and his small action reassured her. If he could pick up on her nonverbal cues, then she knew he would stop if she needed him to.

"If this isn't something you want, we can walk back into the lounge, have a drink—or we can go back down to my office. No questions asked."

He was a good guy, no doubt about it. Jamie shook her head, stepped toward him and placed her hand on his chest, above his heart. "This isn't something I've done for a long, long time but…"

"But?"

"I want to, okay? I'm just not sure how to tell you."

His mouth quirked up at the corners. "You just did."

His smile took her breath away, and when he placed his mouth on hers, his lips were still curved. Then he put just enough distance between their lips for him to speak. "I want you so much, Jamie."

She curled her hand around his neck and stepped closer, pushing herself against him, enjoying the way his hard body complemented hers. Opening her mouth, she fell into his kiss, shocked by the hunger in his eyes. For her.

"You're so much more than what I dreamed," Rowan muttered, clasping the side of her face and tipping her head up. His eyes—the color of a midnight sea—flared with passion. "Can I undress you, take you to bed?"

Knowing what she wanted—him—she didn't hesitate. "Yes. Please."

Jamie heard Rowan's sigh of relief, and she released one of her own when his hands gripped her hips close to his, allowing her to feel the hard length of his erection pushing into her stomach. He lifted his hand, covered her breast and his thumb found her nipple, brushing over it with perfect pressure. He hadn't done much beyond kissing her and her panties were damp.

But if he didn't kiss her again soon, she would die from frustration. Jamie stood on her tiptoes and slammed her lips onto his, her tongue tracing the seam of his mouth, demanding he open up.

She didn't push like this, Jamie thought from a place far away. Before Kaden, even *with* him, she waited for men to make the first move—to kiss her, to lead. She followed.

But not today.

Rowan made her feel reckless, confident. Powerful.

Rowan held her tightly and let her kiss him. When he didn't open his mouth or kiss her back, Jamie started to pull away.

Rowan growled a harsh "no" and moved his hand from her breast to the back of her head to keep her in place. "I was loving that," he told her. "Your mouth is…heaven."

Then Rowan started kissing her—hot, drugging kisses—and she was lost.

This was why she was here—to experience this. To share this with Rowan. He was a stranger, but she knew him, and he knew her. He knew how to touch her, kiss her, build her up, pull her back. To make her yearn. And burn.

Jamie pulled his shirt from the back of his pants and put her hands on his hot masculine skin. Rowan groaned his approval, and as her palms drifted over his gorgeous ass, she became annoyed at the barrier of clothes between her fingers and his flesh.

Rowan kissed the corner of her mouth, trailed his lips over her jaw, nipped her neck as he slowly stripped her of her clothes. Standing in her bra and panties, she realized it had been a long time since a man had made her feel like she was something infinitely marvelous and ravishing.

And, God, she'd missed this. Missed being in a man's arms. The heat and the strength, the yin and the yang. Needing to touch him, to know every part of him, she stroked his hard shaft with the pad of her finger, from base to tip, and was rewarded by the sound of a low curse.

Needing more, Jamie opened the snap on his pants, pulled down his zipper and released his straining erection from his underwear. Using both hands to hold him, she arched as Rowan nipped and sucked on the tender skin where her neck and shoulder met.

He walked her backward and gently turned her around and asked her to put her hands on the wall. She gasped when his mouth touched every bump on her spine, barely noticing her bra falling to the floor. Stepping close to her, both his hands covered her breasts, his fingers teasing her nipples into hard points.

"I want you," he muttered.

Rowan pulled her panties down; but before she could feel embarrassed about being naked while he was still dressed, his fingers slid in between her legs, finding her bundle of nerves with ruthless efficiency. Jamie was close—she wouldn't be able to hold on—and she started to moan.

He pushed a finger into her, then another, and she climbed…reaching, teetering, desperate.

Rowan pulled his hand away and turned her around to face him. His eyes, rich with desire, held hers as he stripped, and as soon as he was naked—his gorgeous body more muscled than she'd expected—he gripped the back of her thigh and lifted her leg to rest over his hip. She groaned when his erection brushed her sweet spot.

Pulling her backward, Rowan moved toward his enormous bed, pulling her down so her legs fell on either side of his thighs, as close as they could be without him slipping inside.

He rested his forehead against hers. "As wonderful as this feels, we need a condom."

Jamie dragged her core up his erection and smiled when Rowan groaned. "Just give me a minute more."

"I don't have that much patience."

But Rowan gripped her hips and lifted her, the muscles in his stomach and arms contracting. *Whoa. So hot.* He slid inside her, still unsheathed.

He rocked and she closed her eyes, swept away by the feeling of perfection.

Rowan cursed then and pulled out. He gently placed her on the bed and rooted around in the drawer of the bedside table before pulling out a strip of condoms and abruptly ripping one off. He removed the latex without dropping his eyes from hers.

There was something sexy about a guy who engaged in so much eye contact.

He stared down at her, pinning her with all that deep blue. Without asking, Jamie lay back on the cool cotton of his duvet, and her legs fell open. She watched, fascinated, as Rowan rolled on the condom and then lowered his body to cover hers, his erection nudging her opening.

"I can't wait to be inside you."

Jamie touched his jaw with her fingers. "Nobody is asking you to wait," she told him.

He used his hand to test whether she was ready, to tease her a little more, and then he slid inside her, hot and big and wonderful.

And she stepped oh-so-willingly into a giant sparkler, the heat igniting a series of fireworks under her skin. Rowan placed his hand under her butt and yanked her up at the same time he plunged inside, and those individual fireworks amalgamated to create a firestorm, the explosion ripping her apart from the inside out.

It was the best, brightest, most intense orgasm

she'd ever experienced, and no sooner had it died down than she wanted another.

And then another.

Sex with Rowan, she decided as she watched the kaleidoscope of colors dance behind her eyes, was immediately addictive.

That might be a problem.

She'd forgotten how good sex could be.

Jamie lay facedown on Rowan's big bed, one arm dangling off the side, her fingertips resting on the cool hardwood floor. She couldn't move, couldn't think… In fact, she was doing well just to pull air into her lungs.

She was wiped.

And it was all Rowan's fault. He'd flipped her inside out and turned her upside down, and she'd loved every second of it. Every kiss, every slide of his hand, every way he made her body and soul sing. She wouldn't be averse to round three—or four— as soon as she recovered, rehydrated and refueled.

Jamie yawned and her eyelids dropped closed. She gathered one of Rowan's pillows, wrapped her arms around it and hiked up her knee. She'd take a nap. Just a small one…

A gentle hand tapping her sheet-covered butt made her groan. "Go 'way."

Rowan's deep laugh washed over her, and he bent and laid a kiss on the side of her neck. "I see you like to sleep," he teased, his voice in her ear.

She couldn't tell him that she never slept through

the night without a sleeping pill and, because she hated taking drugs, she only averaged around three hours of rest a night. The ghosts of her past, specifically Kaden's, visited her between midnight and four and demanded she replay the events of that life-changing road trip.

Sometimes she did, sometimes she didn't—choosing to read, work or watch a movie instead. But either way, sleep was in short supply.

She rolled and was caged by Rowan's hands on either side of her shoulders. She noticed he'd pulled on a pair of sweatpants and a T-shirt, the hem of his sleeves tight around his biceps. Biceps she'd licked and kissed, amazed at their definition and size. There was no doubt about it: Rowan Cowper was ripped.

Big shoulders and arms; washboard stomach; truly excellent bum; and long, athletic legs. *Yum...*

"If you keep looking at me with those come-to-bed eyes, I'm going to..." He narrowed his eyes as his words trailed away.

"You're going to do what?" Jamie asked, her voice sounding sexier than she'd ever heard it.

"Climb back into bed with you," he reluctantly admitted, his expression rueful.

She was about to ask whether that would be such a bad thing, to tease him a little, but she caught the hint of wariness in his eyes. She didn't blame him for feeling that way. Their connection had been intense, a roller coaster of sensation, and they needed to put some physical and emotional distance between them.

Theirs was only a physical connection, a couple of hours of fun, nothing serious. Jamie sat up and pulled the sheet under her arms. "We made love twice, but it's been a while for me so…"

He nodded, stroked her sheet-covered thigh before standing up. "Absolutely."

Okay, then. Right. She dropped her head, a little embarrassed, thrown off her stride by his quick understanding.

Rowan handed her a T-shirt. "I've opened a bottle of wine. Do you want a glass?"

She looked at him, tipping her head to the side.

Was he just being polite? Should she accept? What if she did and he didn't want her to stay? What were the protocols here? Why wasn't there a standard policy for these types of situations?

"It's a glass of wine, Jamie, not an invitation to move in," Rowan stated wryly.

She shrugged and felt her face heat. "I don't know how to act. I feel like I should go."

"Why?"

"I'm not sure if you want me to stay or whether you're being polite," Jamie admitted.

"I'm never polite. Ask anyone. And I asked you to stay because I'd like you to share a glass of wine with me. And if we can still stand each other after an hour, I'll ask you to share a pizza with me. And if we are still enjoying each other's company after that, I'm going to ask you to come back to bed with me. And then I'll make you scream. Again."

"I did not scream," Jamie said. Kaden had always

said she was incredibly silent during sex. "I'm not a screamer, moaner or whimperer."

"Trust me, you did all three," Rowan assured her as he stood up and walked out of the room.

Jamie flopped back on the pillow and covered her eyes with her forearm. She'd had a one-night stand, and she'd liked it. She'd been uninhibited enough to let go, to verbalize her pleasure. She'd felt comfortable enough to explore Rowan's gorgeous body with her teeth and her tongue, had allowed him access to her body after a couple of brief conversations. Somehow she'd temporarily left her guilt and grief at Rowan's bedroom door. She didn't recognize herself…and neither would anyone else.

Maybe, just this once, that was a good thing.

Four

Hearing her footsteps on his living room floor, Rowan poured some red wine into his glass and placed the bottle back on the coffee table. He sat on one of the lounge chairs next to his plunge pool, his legs stretched out, feeling lazy and, for once, stress free.

Early-evening sex was the bomb.

He watched out of the corner of his eye as Jamie stepped onto his private balcony and heard her gusty sigh. He knew why: his view of downtown Annapolis and Spa Creek from his apartment was kick-ass. He loved his three-bedroom apartment and sometimes couldn't believe that he—the kid from the worst suburb in Chicago, the kid who ran wild, boosted cars, shuffled from foster home to foster home—now owned various buildings on the East Coast, including this one.

Rowan watched as Jamie walked over to the infinity railing and rested her arms on the top, the fabric of his shirt riding up as she bent forward, showing him a glimpse of her panties. Of course she'd put on panties; he couldn't quite imagine her walking around commando, especially outside.

Jamie acted sophisticated, but he suspected that underneath the glossy hair and expertly made-up face was a woman with unexplored depths. She wasn't fragile or brittle, but he sensed she had demons nipping at her heels.

Don't they all?

"Your place is fantastic," Jamie told him, turning to face him.

"Thanks. I like it," Rowan replied, standing up. He picked up her glass of wine and walked it over to her. He gestured to the plunge pool. "Feel free to jump in. The water's warm."

"Naked?" Jamie asked, a hint of shock in her eyes.

Rowan tapped his bare foot against the transparent panels. "Clear looking out, opaque looking in. Nobody could see you from down below, and no one can look at you from up above." He looked up and squinted. "Maybe helicopters, birds and satellites."

"Funny," Jamie replied after sipping her wine. "Thanks, but I'll pass."

Rowan sat down again on the two-seater lounge chair and patted the space next to him. After a moment of internal debate, she sat down next to him, rearranged his shirt so she kept her decency and leaned back with a contented sigh, her small shoulder resting against his. "This is nice."

"It is."

A few minutes passed, and Rowan turned his head to see if she'd fallen asleep again. He smiled when he saw that her head was back and she was staring at the few stars in the now-black sky. She looked relaxed and content, and he was happy to see her that way. "Why did you come over tonight? I never expected to see you again."

She rolled her head to look at him. "I came to drop off your tuxedo jacket. I had it dry-cleaned."

"Very thoughtful of you, but we both know you could've had it delivered."

He half smiled at her busted look. Jamie sipped from her wineglass, her fall of hair blocking his expression from her view. "Why, Jamie? And is Jamie your full name or a nickname, by the way?"

"James Jessamy is my full name, but Greg shortened it to Jamie."

"Not JJ?" Rowan asked and grinned when annoyance jumped into her eyes.

"Not if you want to keep living."

He grinned once more before returning to the subject at hand. "So, your impromptu visit?"

"You're like a dog with a bone," Jamie muttered.

"It's been said," Rowan replied, not offended. Determination had gotten him his first job and kept him going when he lost money on his first solo building gig. It had helped him grow his business despite numerous cash flow crises, bad faith suppliers, and con men wannabe investors.

Jamie placed her wineglass on the side table next to her and clasped her linked hands between her thighs. "I'll admit, the tux jacket was just an excuse to see you. I'm not sure why, because I promise I'm not looking for a relationship."

She'd said that before, in the elevator. Then, like now, his curiosity was piqued. He knew why he wasn't interested in anything long-term—to him, love meant being let down, being abandoned, and he vowed he'd never be disappointed like that again. But something about Jamie made him think she should be married and have kids, and that she belonged in a permanent relationship.

He'd known many women in his life, knew how to read them. He could tell who was greedy, who was clingy, who needed constant love and assurance. He sensed that Jamie functioned best when she was one-half of a whole.

Her brow was furrowed, and Rowan knew she either didn't want to answer him or couldn't, so he asked another question. "Earlier, downstairs, you were zoned out. What were you thinking about?"

"Ah, um… I have a client who keeps asking me out. He's being unusually persistent."

Mmm-hmm. He didn't believe her. She'd looked too sad and too lost to have been thinking about some dude she didn't want to date.

"I was also thinking about my mom and her campaign to find me a man—oh, shit!"

Her eyes widened and she grabbed his right wrist, turning it so that she could see his watch. Then she swore again. "Oh, I'm in such big trouble."

"What's the problem?" Rowan asked.

"I missed dinner at my parents' house!" Jamie muttered, leaping to her feet. "Where's my bag? I need my phone. In another half hour, they are going to start calling hospitals and morgues."

Right, that seemed like an overreaction. She was around thirty, give or take—a grown woman. "Your phone is downstairs, in my office."

She swore again and rocked from foot to foot. "Can I run down to get it?"

"You could, but if you know your folks' home number, you can just use my phone." He picked up his phone from the side table and handed it over.

Jamie sent him a thankful glance. "Thank you. And, yes, I do know the number." She punched in the digits, and he heard the call ring through.

A squawking voice came from the other end of the line. "Are you okay? Are you hurt? You're ninety minutes late!"

Jamie gripped the bridge of her nose with her thumb and index finger. "Sorry, Mom, I was… I am… My phone died."

God, she was a terrible liar. "And I got held up at work," she added.

Squawk, squawk.

He listened to her end of the conversation. "I'm sorry I worried you, Mom…No, I'm not coming over…It's been a long day…I'll talk to you soon…"

Her mom wasn't ready to let her end the conversation. "Dinner? Maybe next week…Got to go, Mom…No, I didn't watch *The Bachelor*…Mom, I've *got* to go. Love you."

When she was done, Jamie smacked his phone on her forehead a couple of times before handing it back to him. "Thanks. My mom worries if she doesn't know where I am."

"I gathered," Rowan stated. Leaning across, he picked up her wineglass and pushed it into her hand. "Drink."

Jamie took a few sips and eventually sat down on the edge of the lounge chair, draping one long leg over the other.

"Why the panic?" Rowan asked after she'd taken a few more sips. "You're an adult and fully capable of looking after yourself."

"I am and I do, but there's a reason, a good one, why they worry." She shook her head. "And, no, we're not getting into that tonight."

He saw the stubborn look in her eye, the way her chin lifted, and realized that there would be no budging her on that topic now. He'd retreat and circle back if she gave him the opportunity. "Tell me about your client, the one who keeps asking you on a date."

"His name is Drake, and he's pretty persistent."

Rowan tasted something sour at the back of his throat. The thought of her dating someone else, sleeping with someone else, made his skull shrink, his skin tighten. He wasn't the jealous type, so he couldn't understand what it was about this woman that threw him off his stride. Not only did he feel jealous but he also wanted to know more, to dig and delve into her life and explore her fascinating personality.

He didn't recognize himself.

Jamie didn't offer any further explanations and her reticence was strangely, and ironically, frustrating. Maybe if he opened up, just a little, she would too. Yeah, he was definitely becoming a stranger to himself.

"I know how that feels… My ex-fiancée keeps asking me for another chance."

Her amazing eyes connected with his. "And you don't want to give her one?"

"I'd rather shove my head into a vat of concrete," he replied. "She left me because I wasn't taking her to fancy parties and because we didn't live in a mansion on the water. She wanted unlimited access to my cash and walked out on me when I wouldn't give it to her."

Jamie winced.

"I didn't have unlimited cash back then. I was mortgaged to the hilt, trying to get a project done on time and facing late-delivery penalties. I was barely keeping my head above water." This was information he'd never shared with anyone, but he couldn't keep the words behind his teeth.

Jamie rested her wineglass on her knee. "Let me guess—you did deliver on time, and had she held on for a couple of months, she would've been living on easy street."

He smiled at her accurate summation of the situation. Not about living on easy street, but he had made a helluva killing on that deal. From then on, the cash and projects had started flowing in.

"She's seen pictures of me, in the papers and online, attending these A-list events, and she's angling to reconnect, to get in on that action."

"Have you told her that the food portions are terrible and the company can be a bit handsy?" Jamie asked, amusement in her eyes.

"I don't talk to her at all, but the texts and emails keep rolling in."

Jamie wrinkled her nose. "And I suppose you can't change your email address or phone number because they are linked to your business?"

He nodded.

"It's difficult when the lines between business and personal become blurred."

Difficult and annoying. And time-consuming. He routinely worked sixteen-hour days and had enough to deal with without weeding out unwelcome emails and deleting text messages. Besides, *over* meant *over*. When and how would she get the message?

"You have a clingy ex, and I have a persistent admirer…"

Rowan sent Jamie a sharp glance, wondering where she was going with that statement.

"And…?" he asked her, sounding wary.

She sent him a quick look, obviously picking up on his chary tone, and he wondered what was coming next. What he didn't expect was her laughter, or how the joyful sound danced on the summer air and made his head spin. Women didn't normally make him feel off-center, but she did. She also made his hands itch to touch her, his mouth needed to be on hers and, yeah, he needed to slide inside her...

She felt like home.

An asinine thought because a woman couldn't be home. No person could.

"Relax. Despite you rocking my world, I'm not about to make any demands on you. I'm not interested in a relationship."

He'd rocked her world? He knew she'd had fun—he made sure his partners enjoyed sex as much as he did—but "rocking someone's world" was a helluva compliment. So, yeah, he'd take it.

To mask his confusing reaction of disappointment and relief—relief he understood, but he had no idea why he was feeling disappointed—he slapped a hand on his chest. "I'm wounded."

"No, you're not. You don't want a relationship either."

Jamie leaned back and looked up at the sky. His heart kicked up as he took in the pretty picture she made—dressed in only his T-shirt, bare legs, incredible eyes and messy hair, smelling all feminine and wonderful. The woman short-circuited his brain.

"Do you want to see me again?" Jamie asked, placing her hand on his leg and squeezing. "We can keep it light, on the surface, enjoy each other in bed. And out."

She sounded like she was ordering coffee, giving directions to a cab driver, speaking to a stranger—

calm, cool and under control—and it pissed him off. Dear God, his emotions—usually buried deep— were wreaking havoc on his heart. He had to get himself under control.

Rowan ran his hand over his jaw, his eyes on the hand she had on his thigh. A couple of inches higher and it would be on his package, and his brain would completely shut down. No one had ever made him lose his shit like this.

Needing to put some distance between them, Rowan stood up and walked over and gripped the railing. He stretched out his arms, looking through the glass panels at the busy street below. The car lights made pretty red, yellow and white streaks as they moved through the city.

He pulled in a few deep breaths and considered Jamie's question. Of course he wanted to see her again, but he didn't know if he should. She had the ability to slide under his skin, make him feel things he shouldn't, mess with his self-control.

He rarely dated, and he never continued seeing anyone, even when there was an intense attraction, whether that attraction was sexual or emotional. His dates, if you could call them that, were always with women he could easily walk away from. He didn't like, or trust, excess of emotion. He didn't want to find himself liking a woman too much, being in the position of craving her company, missing her when she wasn't around. It was human nature to seek companionship—he knew that—but he couldn't allow himself to get used to having someone in his life.

Because people always, always left. And it hurt like hell when they did.

He'd taken one chance in his life, and that was with his ex-girlfriend, Marisa. He hadn't fallen in love with her, but she'd been nice, interesting, bright. She'd told him she wasn't interested in the long term, that she just wanted a fling, but somehow that morphed into her becoming his girlfriend, spending most nights at his place, carving out a place in his life for herself. And he'd thought he could deal. Being one-half of a couple wasn't so bad. In fact, it had been nice to come home to someone after a long day.

He'd been surprised at how much it hurt when he discovered she was cheating on him, how empty his life felt when she left. Not because he missed her, particularly, but he missed not feeling alone. But she—like his mother, like the various foster parents he'd encountered—had made promises that never materialized. Everyone he forged an emotional connection with left.

He was mentally, sexually *and* emotionally attracted to Jamie.

It was a wild chemical reaction, a hunger he'd never experienced before. He had an undistilled physical craving to make her his—lust in its purest form.

But he was old enough to understand that when the chemistry between two people was that powerful, a sexual relationship could morph into something more. And that was why he could only allow himself one night with her. He couldn't risk anything developing between them. It had happened before with Marisa, and she couldn't hold a candle to Jamie.

He did not doubt that loving and losing Jamie would emotionally sideswipe him.

And really, he'd had enough of those types of losses in his life, thanks very much. He had no choice but to protect himself.

"I'm sorry but...no."

He'd said no? What the hell?

Jamie looked at his broad back, took a moment to admire his truly excellent butt and then yanked her thoughts back. No? *Really?* What the hell was wrong with the man?

Jamie stood up and walked over to him so she could see his face. "Are you kidding me?"

His hard expression said he obviously wasn't. Jamie tapped her foot in irritation. She didn't see a problem with them meeting up again. He didn't want a relationship and neither did she. They could keep sleeping together until they tired of each other or one of them wanted to move on.

It was a clever unemotional arrangement that would benefit them both. She couldn't see a downside.

Rowan's expression was implacable. "Sorry," he said, shrugging.

Jamie ignored the knife in her chest that was tearing a hole through her heart. "I thought you enjoyed yourself with me," she stated, proud of her calm voice.

"You know I did."

His cold tone didn't reassure her, and she was immediately assaulted by a wave of doubt. Had she done something wrong? Did he not want a repeat? Was she so out of practice? There was no way she'd let him know she was having doubts about her performance. Of course she was; she hadn't had sex in five years… More, because she and Kaden hadn't been active in the bedroom in the last few months before he died. They'd argued about their fertility issues, and those fights had cast a pall over their sex life.

"I think sleeping together again would make things complicated," Rowan said eventually, and it was obvious he was choosing his words carefully.

Complicated? How? She wasn't asking for more than a few hours in bed. But Jamie was damned if she would continue this conversation. She would not beg. She had more pride than that. But, man, it hurt knowing that she wanted him far more than he wanted her.

It had been stupid to suggest an affair anyway. What had she been thinking? Right…she hadn't been. She'd just been confused by hormones and outstanding orgasms. She liked who she was when she was with Rowan, felt connected to the old Jamie— the person she'd been before life slapped her around.

She held up her hands, forced herself to smile and gestured in the direction of his bedroom. "I'm just going to get changed, and I'll get out of your hair. Thanks for the…"

She stopped, not sure how to continue. *Thanks for*

*my multiple O's? For making me feel like a woman
again? For doing that thing with your tongue?*

"Thanks for the wine," she said, turning away.

Rowan gripped the hem of her T-shirt, stopping
her from stomping inside. She whirled around,
scowling at him. "What?"

"I really did have a good time, Jamie."

She nodded and faked a smile. "Me too."

She turned to go back into the bedroom to get
dressed. Pulling on her clothes, she blinked away
her tears, wondering if she'd ever meet another man
who could make her feel the way he did, make her
feel safe and excited, tempted and turned on.

She was probably just the newest entry on his
list of one-night stands, but he was the man who'd
made her feel alive and attractive, feminine and
free, for the first time in years.

Whenever she was with him, she forgot about
her grief and guilt and felt like the best version of
herself. Maybe that was why she wanted to see him
again: with him, she could step out of the past and
into the present.

Whatever the reason, it didn't matter, she thought,
tucking her shirt into her pants and slipping on her
shoes. He didn't want a repeat, and that was his pre-
rogative.

Unfortunately, his rejection hurt far more than
it should. And that was stupid because he was little
more than a stranger.

A stranger she seemed to know all too well.

Five

Come for a family and friends barbecue this Saturday and stay for an outdoor movie. We'll have some time during the socializing to talk business. Bring a date.

Rowan reread the text message that had just landed on his phone from one of Maryland's most successful real estate developers, a man he'd been trying to meet with for months now. They'd shaken hands at social events and exchanged small talk, but every time Rowan had asked for a meeting, he was blown off, with Matt finding one excuse or another.

So a personal invitation to visit Matt's on-the-water property was unexpected and very welcome indeed. Rowan just needed a half hour to pitch his vision of developing the land he owned north of the city into an eco-friendly residential, business and shopping park. Piquing Matt's interest would lead to a formal meeting and, hopefully, a partnership.

Rowan could do the project on his own, and would if he had to, but having someone like Matt—and his marketing machine—on board would boost interest and lead to quicker up-front sales. He didn't *need* Matt, but his involvement would be helpful.

But to pitch his idea, Rowan had to attend the function at Matt's mansion in Whitehall Beach. And he needed to bring a date. Rowan did a mental run-through of the women he could ask, finding fault with each one as he went along. *Too clingy, too political, her laugh sounded like nails on a chalkboard...*

Shit. He wanted Jamie and no one else. And that was just one of the reasons why he was standing in the reception area of her advertising agency without an appointment. But it was the end of the day and, hopefully, she was done. Hey, it had worked for her when she unexpectedly dropped in on him; he was hoping to have the same luck.

He wasn't a guy who blew hot and cold, who played with women, but from the moment she'd walked out of his apartment weeks ago, he'd deeply regretted saying no to her "let's do this again" offer. He had to be the only guy in history to turn down mind-blowing, uncomplicated sex.

Over the time away from her, he'd convinced

himself that he could sleep with her and not allow his emotions to get involved. When a person was aware of the pitfalls, he or she could dodge them. If he kept clear parameters in place—no intense conversations and no sleepovers—he wouldn't make the same mistake he'd made with Marisa, and there would be no chance of him ending up feeling dinged and dented.

As lovely as Jamie was, he wouldn't let himself feel more for her than he should. He refused to watch another person he cared for walk away. Sleeping with her could oh-so-easily lead to authentic dating, and that had to be avoided at all costs.

Unfortunately, he couldn't stop remembering how incredible they were together, and he wanted her back in his bed.

Or in *her* bed, on the floor, up against a wall…

Rowan gave himself a mental slap and told himself *again* that this would only be a fling. He wouldn't cross any lines or allow any lines to be crossed.

All presuming, of course, that she gave him a second chance at saying yes.

He wanted to see her again, wanted her naked under him, but it felt crass to walk into her office and just ask. Luckily, he had an icebreaker—a damn good reason for getting in touch with her once more.

The morning after setting his bed on fire, he'd remembered that Jamie's vintage dress couldn't be repaired, and he felt compelled to spend hours online trying to track down another. But since he knew less than nothing about vintage clothing, he'd gone down various rabbit holes online before admitting defeat. After returning to his senses, he commissioned a vintage-clothing collector to track down a suitable replacement for Jamie's ruined dress.

Thanks to finding a picture online of Jamie wearing the dress at another society event, the collector had a frame of reference. Earlier this week, he heard that she'd tracked down another dress—a little older, a slightly different style, gold instead of silver—and the garment had arrived today. He'd forked out an obscene amount of money for it, and he hoped it fit. And that Jamie liked it.

But, because he didn't want her staff to wonder, and then gossip about why he was giving her a dress, he'd left the garment in his car. He'd hand it over when he could get her alone.

The receptionist cleared her throat to attract his attention. "Ms. Bacall-Metcalfe is currently with someone, Mr. Cowper. And then she needs to leave because she has a dinner engagement across town."

Dinner engagement? The thought of Jamie going out with someone else left a bad taste in his mouth. Jealousy, it turned out, tasted revolting.

The receptionist turned away to answer a call, and he tuned back into her conversation when she mentioned the name Drake. "Despite the many conversations we've had, Mr. Cummings, I really can't call you Drake. And I'm sorry, but Ms. Bacall-Metcalfe is in a meeting. She asked that you direct any queries to our creative director."

So the persistent Drake hadn't given up. Rowan

jammed his hands into his pants pockets and, gritting his teeth, stared past the receptionist's head to an oversize black-and-white photograph of downtown Annapolis.

He had to get himself under control! He had a plan, and he needed to stick to it. He'd give Jamie the dress, ask her to accompany him to Matt's barbecue; and if she said yes—which wasn't guaranteed—he'd then see whether there was any chance of revisiting her offer.

One step at a time...

"Rowan Cowper?"

Rowan turned and saw a masculine version of Jamie walking down the hallway toward him, his hand outstretched. "Hey, I'm Greg Bacall."

Rowan shook his hand, pleased. Greg was the architect he wanted to design his green residential park but hadn't approached yet because he'd hoped to get Matt on board first.

"Are you looking for an ad campaign?" Greg asked.

Ad campaign? "No, actually, I was hoping for a word with Jamie."

Greg's eyebrows rose in surprise. "She's in her office, getting ready to leave. We're going to dinner at my parents' house, and she's dawdling."

Greg jerked his head in a "follow me" gesture, and Rowan fell into step beside him. A minute later Greg knocked on the office door at the end of the hallway and opened it. "You have a visitor."

Jamie, who was zipping up her laptop case, looked up in surprise. "Rowan? What are you doing here?"

"Hi there," Rowan said, stepping into her office. He gave her a quick once-over, and his breath caught in his throat. She wore a short, body-skimming white dress that ended midthigh, and his gaze was immediately drawn to the gold zipper running from her throat to her cleavage.

Sexy. And damn tempting.

Their eyes clashed, held. Within hers, he saw bemusement, embarrassment and, thank God, a healthy dose of desire. At least he wasn't alone in this madness.

She dragged her eyes off his to look past him. "I thought you had gone, Greg."

Rowan turned and caught the smirk on Greg's face. "I was on my way. Then I saw Rowan and decided to come back."

Jamie narrowed her eyes. "You need to fetch Chas, and I'll see you at dinner."

"Dinner *with the parents*," Greg said, emphasizing the words.

Jamie spread out her hands, silently asking him for an explanation.

"Where they'll be discussing, ad nauseam, their thirty-fifth wedding-anniversary party next weekend and demanding to know who you're bringing as your date. So here's a suggestion…ask Rowan to be your date," Greg added.

Jamie released a low growl. "Go away, Gregory."

Greg winced. "Going." He held out his hand to Rowan. "Hope to see you again. We must talk buildings some time."

"I'd like that," Rowan replied, nodding.

"Maybe at the party next weekend," Greg said, winking at Jamie.

A pen flew past Rowan's nose toward the door, but Jamie missed Greg's head by a foot or two. She shook her head and sat down on the edge of her desk. "Sorry about that, Greg has all the subtlety of a sledgehammer." She gripped the edge of her desk and tipped her head to the side. "Why are you here, Rowan?"

"I need a date for a barbecue this Saturday. Would you come with me?" he asked, biting the bullet.

"I thought you didn't want to see me again," Jamie stated.

He ignored her flat tone and kept going. "So I was thinking—"

"Did you hurt yourself?" Jamie asked, her voice sweet but her eyes cool. Her words hardly had time to settle before she waved her hands in the air. "That's not fair, sorry." She pulled her bottom lip between her teeth. "You had every right to turn down my clumsy offer. Sorry, it's been a while, and I'm out of practice."

"It wasn't clumsy, Jamie. It was up-front and honest, and I appreciate that. Admittedly, it was unexpected."

She waved the words away and placed her hands

on her hips and tipped her head to the side. "So what exactly are you asking, Rowan?"

"Will you be my date on Saturday? I'd like to spend a few hours with you… No pressure and no expectations." That sounded loose and casual, didn't it? Pity he didn't feel that way.

Strangely, whether they slept together again or not, right now a few hours of her company was enough. Right. That was a first. "Come with me, eat some great barbecue and watch an outdoor movie."

"Mmm."

Rowan caught himself rocking on his heels, the action suggesting he was anxious to hear her answer…

Curious? Sure. But anxious? Not a chance.

That was what he was telling himself, at least.

"I'll come to your barbecue thingy on Saturday if you come to my parents' anniversary party."

He felt a flash of pleasure at her response and then jerked when her words sank in. *Parents? Family? Oh, hell no!* Family functions were a nightmare. He felt his throat close. Having never had a family of his own, he didn't *do* families.

He cleared his throat, desperately looking for a decent excuse until he pushed a question past his lips. "Surely you don't want a virtual stranger at your family event?"

She raised her eyebrows. "You're looking a bit flustered, Cowper. Haven't you met a girl's parents before?"

Actually, no. Marisa had been estranged from

her parents, and his previous relationships had never gotten to the meeting-the-parents stage. He'd never allowed them to.

"Won't they get the wrong idea?"

Jamie rolled her eyes. "It doesn't matter if they do, because we both know the truth—neither of us wants a relationship! But, yes, maybe if they see that I'm dating, they might stop with the 'it's time you moved on' speeches!"

Now he was very curious. "Moved on from what?"

"So will you come?" she asked, ignoring his question.

He knew that if he said no, she would tell him she was unavailable on Saturday night. And as much as he wanted to talk to Matt, he didn't want to be the lone male surrounded by happy couples and kids.

She had him between a rock and a hard place and, judging by the amusement in her eyes, she knew it.

"I'm not the meet-the-family type," he warned her.

"Relax," Jamie told him. "You're not facing a shooting squad." She grinned. "An inquisition, maybe, but not a firing squad. Do we have a deal?"

He nodded. "We have a deal."

They were trading one date for another—a simple arrangement. So why did he feel like he was tiptoeing through a minefield?

Jamie gestured to the door. "Great. Not meaning to rush you, but I do have to leave."

If she was in a hurry, then now would be a great time to hand over the dress with minimal explanations. She could examine it later, when he wasn't around. Flora, the woman who found the dress for him, had nearly put him in a coma talking about beads and bodices, skirts and sequins, and he now knew more about vintage dresses than he wanted to.

"Sure. But can you spare five minutes? I have something for you. It's in my car."

Jamie nodded, popped her head into an office and asked someone to lock up before leading Rowan to the front door. They stepped onto the sidewalk, and he placed his hand on her back to guide her a short distance down the road to where he'd parked his new Lexus LX 570.

"Nice car," Jamie commented, not sounding overly impressed.

"I like it."

Rowan opened the back door and picked up the garment bag that lay across the back seat. After slamming the door shut, he handed the bag to Jamie, who took it, a small frown pulling her eyebrows together.

"What's this?" she asked, puzzled.

He had gotten what he wanted, so it was time to go. Besides, he knew nothing about gifts or how to hand them over, and he'd prefer not to make an ass of himself.

"I'll text you the arrangements for Saturday." He bent his head to kiss her cheek. "Bye, James."

He saw the flash of irritation in her eyes at his

use of her full name and decided he didn't care. Sometimes *James* suited her better than *Jamie* did.

He turned away to open the driver's door to his car, but a feminine hand gripped the back of his shirt, keeping him in place. "Not so fast, mister."

Rowan was acting like a cat on a hot tin roof, and she wanted to know why.

She'd spent too much time thinking about him lately.

It had taken all her willpower not to rock up to his office in the hopes of repeating the fabulous hours she'd spent in his arms. One night with the blasted man wasn't enough.

Rowan shifted on his feet. He was normally so cool and contained; it was weird to see him acting angsty. "Why are you acting weird, Cowper?"

He immediately stilled, and his expression turned inscrutable. "I'm fine." He tapped his expensive watch. "You need to get going. You don't want to be late," he told her. "Where is your car parked?"

His eyes kept darting to the garment bag as if it were radioactive. He very obviously didn't want her opening it now, so that was exactly what she intended to do. She handed him her laptop and tote bag to hold and holding the garment bag up with one hand, she slowly drew down the zipper, sending him a teasing glance. "Did you buy me a dress to replace the one we ripped?"

That dress was irreplaceable, but if she had to choose between a ripped dress and being kissed by him in a stuck elevator, she'd choose the kiss every day.

"Yeah," Rowan muttered.

Really? She hadn't expected him to remember her torn dress, never mind going to the effort of replacing it. Rowan was full of surprises. No doubt the dress would be a 1920s rip-off, but it was the thought that counted.

Jamie pulled one edge of the garment bag aside and stared at the rhinestone-covered silk, her breath leaving her body. There was no way... No damn way.

"Oh. My. God."

"I know it's not the same style or color, but the vintage clothing dealer assured me it was an adequate replacement."

Jamie's eyes flew to his face, and through her shock she noticed the flare of disappointment in his eyes, the way his mouth tightened.

"Adequate? Are you kidding me?" Jamie cried as she took the dress out of the garment bag and watched the rhinestones shimmer in the early-evening light. "God, Rowan, my dress was from an unknown designer. This is an Edward Molyneux!"

He shrugged, obviously clueless.

"He's one of the superstar designers of the twenties. He opened his couture house in 1919 in Paris and then opened several other branches in Europe, including London. He was a true artist, and his clients included aristocracy as well as stars of the stage," Jamie explained.

Rowan's eyes lightened as he started to realize

he'd done well. Or his collector had. But she still couldn't accept his exceptionally generous gift. "Rowan, Molyneux's dresses can be seen in the Metropolitan Museum. This dress belongs there. I can't accept it."

But, man, she wanted to. Owning an Edward Molyneux had been on her bucket list, though she never thought she would.

She looked at the dress again, sighing at the exquisite beading and handwork. The longer strands of beads, dripping off the bottom of the skirt, gave the dress movement, and she could easily imagine a fashionable flapper doing the Charleston in a jazz club in Manhattan or Mayfair. She was instantly in love with the dress, but she absolutely couldn't keep it; so she, very reluctantly, covered it with the garment bag.

She pulled the zipper up and bit down on her bottom lip. Her rabid inner collector wanted to keep the dress, but she knew how expensive it was. Rowan's bank balance would've taken a hell of a hit. And it was at least twenty times more expensive than the dress that had ripped.

"It's a really sweet gesture, Rowan, but I can't keep it."

He stared at her, still holding the bags she'd given him when she took the dress. "Yeah, you can. Because I sure as hell do not need it."

"It's too expen—"

"Do you like it?" Rowan interrupted her.

How could he even ask her that? Hadn't she been

drooling over the dress a minute before? "Of course I do. I love it!"

He shrugged. "That's settled, then." He draped her purse over her shoulder and put her laptop bag in her free hand. "You're going to be late."

"Nothing is settled!" Jamie retorted. "You need to send the dress back and get a refund."

"No can do," Rowan told her, dropping a brief kiss on her cheek. "The seller told me it's nonrefundable. Unless it doesn't fit you…"

Jamie's mouth dropped open in horror. "It's way too precious to wear!"

Rowan flashed her a small smile as he pulled open the door to his vehicle. "I'd still like to see you in it. See you on Saturday, James."

He climbed into his car and slammed the door shut. Frustrated, Jamie knocked on his window, and when it slid down, she glared at him. "Rowan, I'm not done discussing this! I don't think you understand the importance of—"

As he grinned at her, the window slid up and he started the car. He smoothly pulled onto the road and left her standing on the sidewalk, holding her bags and an exceedingly expensive and rare vintage dress.

Which she now owned.

And when Rowan's car disappeared, she did a quick but furious happy dance on the sidewalk.

Six

After parking his car, Rowan walked around the hood to open her door and held out his hand. Jamie saw the spark of appreciation in his eyes, and she, foolishly, preened a little as his gaze skimmed over her sexy, blindingly white summer dress. The bodice was lace. Spaghetti straps flowed over her shoulders and crisscrossed down her back, and when she walked, the soft cotton skirt parted to show off her legs. It was perfect for a beach barbecue, and she felt feminine and sexy.

"You look lovely," Rowan told her.

"You look pretty good yourself, Cowper." And he did. He wore a lightweight steel blue button-down shirt over tailored white shorts and expensive sneakers. A designer pair of sunglasses covered his eyes, and his hair looked more tousled than usual. Casual was a good look on him.

Everything was.

She sighed as she put her hand in his. She wanted his approval, loved seeing the flare of attraction in his eyes, waited for that soft, quick smile. With him, she felt lovely, warm from the inside out, like a desirable woman who could take on the world.

Rowan excited her, made her think—and smile. God, he made her feel. He was smart and hot and successful, but more than that, he was a good man. Someone she could fall for, if she wasn't careful. She refused to do that. She would not risk loving and losing someone again. For a year after Kaden's death, she'd barely functioned. The next year had been a little better; she'd started taking an interest in her business again, and being at work helped keep her mind off her devastating loss. Year three had still been brutally lonely, but then guilt—kept at bay by the strength of her grief—strolled in to keep her company.

The same questions plagued her day in and day out. What if she hadn't started that argument? What if she'd agreed to try again, not given up? She'd failed him, failed *them*, and her punishment had been watching him—and the life they'd planned together—die on that lonely asphalt road.

Years four and five were much the same: she worked, she attended some social functions—normally at her mom's and gran's urging—and tried to win at life as best she could. She dated…

if you could call dinner and a kiss on the cheek at her door *dating*.

Then Rowan strode into her life. A couple of hours in an elevator resulted in a comet-hot kiss. Returning his jacket had led to the raunchiest, most addictive sex of her life.

Sorry, Kaden, but... Yeah. That.

And then Rowan had bought her a Molyneux dress. Yes, it was expensive, but the dress could've been a knockoff and she still would've been impressed. He'd remembered her ripped dress, and while the rip hadn't been entirely his fault, he'd made an effort to rectify the situation. He'd gone to a lot of trouble, and she appreciated and respected that.

Underneath that gorgeous packaging was a nice guy...

Great sex or not, nice guy or not, she and Rowan weren't going anywhere. They *couldn't*. He was openly uninterested in a commitment and so was she. But because he was a good guy underneath that gruff exterior, she had to protect herself against liking him more than she should. She couldn't let that happen. *Like* could lead to *love*, and when *great sex* was part of the equation, it sped up the process.

Although she loved being with him, and she'd been the one to originally suggest they continue, she didn't think she was blasé enough for a no-strings affair. When he took her home tonight, she would be strong and tell him she couldn't see him again, that she wasn't ready to dive into an affair.

He'd understand, and if he didn't, well, he'd just have to live with it. She wasn't brave enough to love and lose someone again.

"Are you okay?" Rowan asked, his fingers lightly resting on her bare lower back as he led her up the path to the enormous lakeside mansion.

She stopped, looked up at him and shook her head. If they had this conversation now, they'd be at odds for the rest of the evening, and it would be awkward and uncomfortable. She took a breath and pulled up a smile.

"I'm fine. Let's go in and have a good time, okay?"

His eyes lightened, and his mouth lifted into that half smile, half smirk that made her tummy flutter. "Thanks for coming with me."

Jamie slid her hand into the crook of his arm and held up her floor-skimming dress as they walked up the wide steps leading to the open front door. As they stepped into the hall, a waiter holding a silver tray offered them a cocktail—a classic piña colada, judging by the color, decorated with two colorful paper umbrellas.

She took one; Rowan didn't. She raised her eyebrows at him in a silent question.

"I make it a point to stay away from fruity paint-strippers," he told her as they glanced around the overdecorated double-volume hall. Looking beyond the floating marble staircase, Jamie saw a set of wide open doors leading to an entertainment area filled with people. Her eyebrows raised again when a tanned blonde dressed in a tiny bold-pink thong bikini walked through the doors.

Right. Maybe Jamie was a little overdressed.

"So what's the plan?" she asked Rowan, who, to his credit, barely gave the busty blonde any attention.

"I've been trying to get an appointment with Matt Blunt, and he keeps blowing me off. But he told me he'd spare some time for me tonight."

She rolled through her mental database, then pulled up Matt's face and the few details she knew about him. He was a good guy but rarely did business with anyone outside of a handful of trusted associates. Rowan would need to work hard to break into Matt's inner circle.

Matt was on wife number three, a woman who was quite a lot older than him, French and shy. Matt was protective of her, a collector of vintage watches and a coach for his grandson's Little League team.

"After we circulate a little, we'll find his wife, Odile, and make nice. Trust me, he'll soon come to you."

He sent her an appraising look and nodded. "You do know your way around Annapolis's social scene."

She did. Not as well as her parents did, obviously, but well enough. And she'd learned so much from Kaden. He'd been the life and soul of every party, the guest everyone wanted to talk to, wanted to know. He'd loved this world—the buzz of socializing, the high that came from being in the know.

Frankly, she'd far prefer to be at home, drinking a glass of wine and polishing off a pizza.

She blamed her family for bullying her into going to events, but she knew that wasn't completely fair; they never hassled her when she gave them an unequivocal no. The question remained: Why did she still accept invitations to functions with people she barely knew and sometimes didn't like? Because it was something Kaden loved? Because these people were a link to the life she'd had with him? Because socializing with the A-list was what her family did?

Or maybe it was because if she attended the occasional function, she could convince herself she wasn't lonely, that she *did* have a social life. That she wasn't still grieving her husband, their marriage and the life they'd planned on having.

Was she simply conning herself?

The thing was, after having slept with Rowan, being around Rowan, she felt more alive than she had even before Kaden's death. Since meeting Rowan, she was more in tune with her surroundings; the sky was bluer; the air, softer; the fruit tasted sweeter.

And because there was always a yin to the yang, her attraction to him made her feel scared. And when she wasn't with him, her solitude—normally a protective friend—felt oppressive. Him dropping into her life made her realize how much she'd isolated herself, how lonely she was.

But he didn't want a relationship, and she was too scared to have one. So where did that leave them?

Precisely nowhere.

She'd acted impulsively when she suggested to him, weeks ago, that they have an affair. She wouldn't hold him to their agreement that he attend her parents' party with him, so this would be their first and only date.

But maybe it was time to live again, just a little. Maybe she could open herself up a bit more, and she could reach out to her old girlfriends, wonderful women she'd pushed away when Kaden died. Maybe she could join a book club, accept some of those "women in business" lunch invitations she always declined.

She'd never fall in love again, but maybe she could have friends.

Jamie sipped her drink and wrinkled her nose at the odd taste on her tongue.

"Everything okay?" Rowan asked her.

She lifted the glass to smell her drink. "It tastes and smells funny."

Rowan took the glass from her, smelled it and sipped. "Pineapple, coconut, rum." He shrugged. "It tastes as it should."

He tried to hand it back, but she shook her head. "I can't. I'm sorry. I smell it and I want to gag."

He looked around for a waiter and caught the eye of one, and within seconds, he was by their side. Rowan handed him the glass and asked Jamie what she preferred to drink. She winced. "Some cold water?"

The waiter nodded and looked at Rowan. "A light

beer, thanks," Rowan said as they stepped onto the enormous entertainment deck that was heaving with people.

Jamie looked around, taking in the lavish surroundings. Three pools dotted the lush yard, one holding a ten-foot waterfall and a massive slide. Rowan gestured to the waterfall. "The pools are connected by underwater tunnels."

"Nice," Jamie replied as two young kids disappeared behind the falling water. "Especially for the kids."

Rowan looked down at her. "Fun for all ages. Did you bring your bathing suit?"

"I did not," Jamie replied as they walked down the steps to the fake beach that led into the pool. Matt stood in the center of a group of gorgeous people, all of them dressed in board shorts or bikinis. His wife, wearing a conservative cover-up, stood a little apart from them, looking uncomfortable.

Jamie's heart went out to her. She was on intimate terms with feeling alone. Ignoring the boisterous group, she went straight up to Odile and put out her hand. "We've never met, but I believe you know my mom, Haley Bacall? I'm Jamie and this is Rowan Cowper."

Rowan greeted her in what sounded like fluent French. Odile's face immediately brightened, and she machine-gunned her reply. Rowan listened intently, nodded and spoke again. As they conversed, Jamie wondered where he'd learned to speak the language.

There was so much she didn't know about him.

And, she reminded herself, she never would. She pushed her surge of disappointment away, reluctantly accepting that was the way it had to be. She couldn't take another chance on another man. Her heart couldn't stand it.

A blast of cold water on her back yanked Jamie out of her reverie. She spun around to see a little boy holding a water gun. A red-haired girl raced past her and nailed the boy with a stream of water in his face.

Good job, honey. But Jamie still had a wet back, and a stream of water was heading south...

Rowan immediately whipped a towel off a nearby chair and turned her around, rubbing the water off her skin. "Are you okay?"

She smiled at his concern. "Fine. It's only water."

"I'm so sorry, Jamie. You got caught between a battle that has been raging all day," Odile told her in accented English. "Those two are my oldest grandchildren—the son of my daughter and daughter of my stepson. Mortal enemies."

"No harm done," Jamie assured her.

Odile smiled at her. "Thank you for being so understanding. If you'll excuse me?"

They nodded, greeted Matt, were introduced to his group of friends and received their drink order from the waiter they'd spoken to earlier. The conversation resumed but was frequently interrupted by the shrieks and yells of the kids in the pool and a boom box the teenagers had set up by another pool.

Within minutes, Matt suggested they move back

up onto the entertainment deck so they could hear themselves think.

"That's better," Rowan said after tipping his beer bottle to his mouth. "God, kids are noisy."

"That they are," Jamie replied, raising her eyebrows when a group of preteen boys pushed three posing girls off their pool chairs. They came out of the water cursing and spluttering.

"War has been declared," Rowan said with a grin. He gestured to a pair of toddlers—both wearing inflatable armbands, their mothers close by—who were splashing around at the water's edge.

"Do you like kids? Do you want them?"

It was a question she hated. One she routinely lied about. Most of her and Kaden's friends, all of whom had babies and toddlers, had thought she and Kaden struggled with infertility, and Jamie had found their pity, and condescension, hard to swallow.

They'd never had difficulty getting pregnant. Every time they tried, she conceived right away. No, conception was easy—but *keeping* the baby was something she'd never managed to do.

For her, pregnancy was a roller coaster of hope and expectation, then grief and despair when she inevitably miscarried. After she lost baby number four, she was done. She told Kaden she couldn't put herself through that again. She'd started to tell people, in the months leading up to Kaden's death, that they'd changed their minds about having children, that they were happy to be childless.

Lying served her well back then, so she shrugged.

"You asked me that before," she reminded him. "No, I'm not interested. They are not on my agenda."

She didn't ask his opinion on having children, as it wasn't a subject that would ever affect her. Needing a distraction, she saw Odile slipping into the house and remembered Rowan's excellent French.

"Where did you learn French?" she asked, changing the subject.

"Movies."

"Movies?"

"Yeah."

"I'm going to need a bit more of an explanation than that, Rowan."

He jammed his hands into the back pockets of his tailored shorts. He looked around as if checking whether or not anyone could hear their conversation. "One of my foster mothers was French Canadian and had a bunch of French movies on DVD. I watched a few and got hooked on them. From there, I rented more movies and started reading French books, and I got better. A few years ago, I went to France and realized that I picked up more than I thought. I'm not fluent but I can converse."

He certainly could. As interested as she was in his ability to speak the sexy language, she was more curious about the nugget of information he'd dropped about being a foster kid. "How long were you in the system?"

His eyes cooled and his expression tightened. "Between the ages of four and eleven, I was in and out. I became a permanent resident about six weeks after my twelfth birthday and left, as we all do, when I was eighteen."

There were a million questions she wanted answered, but his flat eyes and rigid mouth suggested she not pry further. Still, she was never any good at following suggestions. Or orders. "Why did you go into foster care? What happened?"

"That's something I don't discuss, James."

Ouch. Jamie winced. Right. His past was a subject he didn't want to discuss. Neither was hers, so fair enough.

Jamie heard Matt calling Rowan's name from the door leading into his house. Rowan lifted his hand in acknowledgment and turned back to Jamie. "Looks like I'm getting my meeting sooner than I expected. Will you excuse me for a half hour or so?"

Jamie nodded. "Sure."

Rowan looked around. "Will you be okay? I don't like leaving you on your own."

That was sweet. "Rowan, there are at least a dozen people I know. I grew up in this world, remember?"

He pushed his hand through his hair and nodded. "Okay. I'll come find you when I'm done."

She nodded and watched him walk away—so confident, so masculine, so at ease in his big, surprisingly graceful body. Jamie glanced at her bracelet watch and grimaced. She rather resented Matt taking Rowan away, because if she was going to end their association later tonight, then she only had a few hours left with him. After he dropped her off at her place, she would relegate him to being a nice guy she'd once slept with, someone who cracked open the seams of her heart and let in a little light.

Just a little.

And that was more than she could cope with.

After he met with Matt, Rowan felt like he was dancing on air. In his direct, no-nonsense way, Matt all but promised—subject to the numbers checking out—that he'd invest in Rowan's project. Matt was impressed by how far Rowan had come in such a short time. Matt said he'd had his eye on him for ages, that it was past time he was involved in an eco-friendly project.

They'd shaken hands and Rowan instinctively knew an agreement had been reached as soon as their hands connected. Oh, contracts would be drawn up and haggled over, but the deal, sealed by that handshake, was in place.

He needed a drink, to celebrate. More than that, he needed to share his good news with Jamie.

About to walk down the shallow steps to the grassy area where Jamie stood with a group of young mothers, he stopped abruptly. Did he need to tell Jamie? Why?

For the past fifteen years, he'd been celebrating his successes solo, and he was very used to enjoying the quick high, then tucking his pride away and getting on with the job. Because he'd never had anyone to celebrate his successes with or to commiserate with when he failed, he simply put his feet back on the ground or picked himself up and carried on.

Yeah, sure, it was lonely, but he was used to it.

Yet seeing her standing there, her expression full of wonder as she gently stroked the cheek of the sleeping baby she held in her arms—bullshit, she didn't want kids!—he wanted to grab a bottle of champagne, swing her up in his arms and fall into her eyes. Eyes that would be misty with excitement for him.

She was the type who would celebrate her partner's successes or support a man when things weren't going as planned. She was a woman who'd pull her weight.

God, he liked her. More than he'd liked any woman, ever. Yeah, yeah, lust was there—she was gorgeous; how could he not want her?—but *like* was so much more dangerous.

He hadn't liked many people in his life. And because he liked her too much, he should let her go.

But he wasn't going to. Not yet.

Jamie handed the baby back, said something to the moms that made them laugh and stepped away. She caught his eye and nodded to the path leading down to the beach. Rowan grabbed a bottle of champagne from an ice bucket and two flutes off the table. He exchanged pleasantries with the other guests as he walked past groups huddled around the pool. Stepping onto the beach, he admired the two long piers and the sleek boat preparing to take guests—mostly teenagers—for a ride. A teenage boy put his cap on back to front, zipped up a life jacket and jumped off the boat into the water. A wakeboard followed him, and the kid slid his feet into the footholds, expertly attaching himself to the board.

Rowan watched as the boat slowly backed away and chugged into deeper water. Another boy tossed the kid a rope; thumbs-up signs were exchanged between the two. Ten seconds later, the kid was skimming across the lake on the board, flying from one side of the boat to the other, doing trick turns and showing off.

At eighteen, Rowan had been too busy trying to survive, finish high school, feed himself, pay the rent. Did the kid have any idea how lucky he was?

"Are you going to drink that or just hold it?"

Rowan poured the champagne into the flutes, handed Jamie one and gestured to the wooden bench on a small knoll. They sat down, and Rowan placed the champagne bottle between them. "You persuaded Matt to invest," she stated, sounding completely confident.

He grinned and tapped his glass against hers. "I did."

Jamie congratulated him before tipping her head to look at him, her eyes cutting through to his soul. "You should smile like that more often. You have a hell of a smile, Cowper."

He blinked, caught off guard. He did? Well, then. "Thank you."

"I'm happy for you, Row."

Row? He'd never liked to hear his name shortened, but he didn't mind it on her lips. He was making all sorts of excuses for her, though that could be because he was happy, excited, he'd had good news. Later, he'd go back to being his cynical self.

"Now that I have Matt's buy-in, I can approach Greg and see if he wants to take my rough drawings and turn them into something workable."

Her eyebrows lifted, and pleasure curved her lips. "You want to work with Greg?"

"I'm *going* to work with Greg," Rowan corrected her. "I called him the day before yesterday and mentioned the project to him. He told me he'd come on board when I have my investor in place. Investor in place. So, yeah, Greg will be my architect."

"Nice," Jamie said before lifting her glass to her lips and sipping. He watched her frown, lower her glass and squint at the bubbly liquid. "This doesn't taste good."

It was the second time he'd given her a drink she hated. Needing to check, Rowan took another sip and shook his head. "It's great champagne, Jamie."

She frowned and looked at her glass again. Her face turned white, and her stunning eyes looked huge in her shocked face.

"What? What is it?"

"Hand me your phone..." she demanded, her voice shaky. "Mine is in my bag on the entertainment deck."

Rowan pulled his phone from his back pocket and handed it over. Why did she need his phone? Who was she going to call?

She punched in some numbers, listened to the phone ring, and when it was answered, Jamie didn't bother with a greeting. "When was your anniversary dinner? At the end of May, right?"

Rowan heard Greg's clear yes, followed by a "Why?" before Jamie abruptly disconnected the call without further explanation. She then thrust his phone at him and told him to open up his calendar. Seeing the wild look in her eyes, he did as she asked, hoping he'd get an explanation.

Jamie poked her finger at the screen, cursing as she did so. Then she repeated the process, her curse words becoming louder.

He placed his glass next to the bottle and folded his arms. "Want to tell me what has you in such a dither?"

Jamie placed her hand on her stomach and shook her head. "Dear God, how?"

How what? What was going on?

Jamie rubbed her hands up and down her face. "I just did a couple of mental calculations, and I don't know how to tell you this but—"

He hated it when people prefaced an announcement with those words. "Just tell me, James!" he snapped, frustrated.

Jamie bent over and rested her face between her knees. She mumbled something, and Rowan demanded that she repeat herself.

Jamie turned her head to the side, her eyes wide. "I think I'm pregnant. And since you're the only person I've had sex with in a long, long time, you're the father."

Seven

Jamie kept her face buried in her knees, needing a few more minutes to stabilize her thoughts and emotions. She fought the urge to look at Rowan's screen again, to count the weeks, hoping and praying she'd made a mistake.

She hadn't. She was three weeks late, and she was never late.

Jamie did a body check, thinking back on the past couple of weeks. She'd been a little tired, but nothing serious. She'd had no morning sickness, and her breasts felt perfectly fine. But, like before, her taste and smell were affected. During her other pregnancies, she'd never been able to tolerate the taste of alcohol.

And, big clue—she was three weeks late. Three freaking weeks!

Jamie sat up slowly, her elbows on her knees and her head in her hands. Gathering all her courage, she looked at Rowan, who was staring at her like she was one of the walking dead.

"Would you like to run that by me again, please? I thought I heard you say that you are pregnant."

Jamie sat up and nodded. "Yeah, I think I am."

"'Think'?" Rowan demanded.

"Well, I can't be sure without a test but, yeah, there's a damn good chance."

Rowan released a harsh curse. "You are shitting me, right?"

She wished she was. She didn't want to have a child with a man she'd planned to never see again. A man who made her feel jittery, like she wasn't sure which way was up. "I wouldn't joke about something like that."

"But... But...we used condoms."

They had.

"Except for that one time, that first time. You slid inside me without a condom."

"I didn't come!" Rowan protested.

"You didn't need to," Jamie told him before waving his words away. In between losing babies two and three, she'd done a lot of research trying to find out why she couldn't stay pregnant. Along the way, she'd discovered other bits of baby-making knowledge, including the fact that ejaculation wasn't the only vehicle for sperm. But she didn't think Rowan would appreciate a lecture on super-super-safe sex. The deed was done...

"The *how* isn't important—"

"It's pretty important to me," Rowan replied, looking stubborn. "How do I know that you didn't sleep with someone else and now are trying to pin this pregnancy on me?"

Jesus, really? Jamie started to blast him, tasted the hot words on her tongue, but then she caught the fear in his eyes, his absolute bewilderment. She swallowed, and clenched and unclenched her hands.

"You are the only guy I've slept with since my husband died, Cowper—"

"You were married? How did I not know this?" he demanded.

"We haven't spent that much time together, Rowan. And the time that we did spend together, we didn't talk much."

"Fair point," he conceded, rubbing his jaw.

"Anyway, the last time I had sex was with my husband, and he died about five years ago. So, yes, if I am pregnant, the baby is yours."

Rowan rested his forearms on his knees and dangled his hands between his legs. He now looked as pale as she imagined she did. "I didn't even know that you were married, that you are a widow. And now you're telling me you're pregnant. I'm trying to process everything at once."

Jamie resisted the urge to put her hand on his back, to tell him that they'd get through this together, that he didn't need to overreact. Now that the shock was starting to recede, she could think. She had a little human growing inside her, the baby she'd always wanted—*craved*. Excitement bubbled and then spread its warmth through her veins as sparks danced on her skin...

She was going to be a mother...

Then reality rushed back in—cold, dark and relentless.

Jamie slumped and fell in on herself, her excitement evaporating. There was no need to get excited, no cause to overreact. She knew how this went. She'd lived it before. She'd have a couple of weeks of exhaustion, some morning sickness and then, between weeks ten and twelve, she'd start to bleed.

By week thirteen, all traces of the baby would be gone.

She'd been through this four times before—they called her condition recurrent pregnancy loss—and she had no reason to believe she'd carry this baby full-term. Nobody knew why, but it wasn't something she could do.

She started to tell Rowan, but stopped at the last minute. Maybe she should confirm she was pregnant before confessing that she was bound to lose the baby, that he shouldn't get excited.

If that was what he was...

Scared or weirded out might be more accurate.

Do the pregnancy test, see what it says and then take it from there. Horse before the cart, Jamie. Horse before the cart...

Back at her house, Rowan followed Jamie into her living room—cream walls, bold colors, interesting art—and shoved the brown paper sack into her hands. They'd stopped by the first pharmacy they'd come across, and he'd bought every type of pregnancy test they sold, much to the pharmacy assistant's bemusement. She'd tried to tell him all the tests were pretty accurate these days and that he only needed one, but he'd insisted on buying every brand they stocked. He had ten, twelve different tests in the bag, including a more expensive digital test. Apparently, that one could tell how far along Jamie was.

Jamie looked into the brown bag and raised her eyebrows. "How many did you buy?"

"Do them all," Rowan told her, feeling a little light-headed. He knew he wasn't handling this well, but how was one supposed to handle a pregnancy scare?

"I am not peeing on all these sticks," Jamie stated.

"Can you just go and do it already?" he growled, shifting from foot to foot on her carpet.

Jamie rolled her eyes. "Can I put my bag down, have a cup of tea first?"

He pulled the bag off her shoulder, tossed it onto the nearest chair and jerked his chin toward the hallway.

Jamie threw up her hands, silently admitting defeat. "Okay, I'm going."

She tipped the packet of pregnancy tests onto the coffee table, pushed them around before picking up two boxes. "I'll do two—a standard test and the more expensive one."

He wanted to argue, but saw that she held the digital test in her hand and nodded. Heart in his throat, he watched Jamie walk away, taking in her slim back and rounded hips.

One time? One time and she was pregnant? How the hell did that happen?

And how was he going to handle a child?

Rowan paced the area of her living room agitated. He was a child of the system. He'd never known his real dad, and his mother hadn't had a maternal bone in her body. She'd been constantly looking for the next party, the next man, the next high. Rowan had been, at best, an inconvenience; at worst, a pain in her ass.

When she took off shortly after his twelfth birthday, he hadn't been surprised. When they told him, he was shocked she hadn't done it sooner. But her running away was a pattern that plagued him for the rest of his life. He'd had a teacher he liked but who soon moved on. He'd had a couple who were prepared to adopt him, but they left the state. One of his oldest friends, another kid who grew up in the system with him, was killed in a gang-related shooting.

By the time Rowan had hit his teens, he was cynical. In his twenties that cynicism had hardened to flat-out mistrust. He'd had girlfriends, but no one he allowed into his inner world. Marisa had gotten closer than most, but even she didn't stick around for the long haul.

Now he made damn sure he walked away first. Because he never wanted to watch someone walk away from him again, to be hurt again.

Just like he'd planned to walk away from Jamie at some point in the future.

But now she might be pregnant.

She couldn't be. Surely it took more than a one-night stand to fall pregnant? It had to!

But if she was, how would he handle the situation? He wouldn't repeat his mother's mistake and walk away from his child. Neither could he allow Jamie to raise the baby alone. Dammit! He'd never planned on having kids and had constructed his life so that he'd never be emotionally entangled. If Jamie *was* pregnant, he'd be in a position he'd never wanted, or even imagined, he would be in!

He looked down at his shaking hands and reluctantly admitted that the only silver lining of this situation was that he was in this with Jamie, that his kid would have her as a mom. She was smart, lovely, successful, and she had her life together. If he'd had the option of choosing the mom for his child, she would have been his first and only choice.

Rowan glanced at his watch, impatience building. Wanting to know what the delay was, he walked down the hallway, opening doors. Study, guest bedroom, family bathroom.

At the end of the hallway, he nudged a half-open door with his foot and stepped into a feminine bedroom, white with touches of lavender. The bed was made, but a pile of unfolded laundry sat in the middle of it, along with an open book, facedown.

Her room smelled like she did: lovely and light, sexy and subtle, with a hint of wildness.

"Rowan? Are you in my bedroom?" she asked from her en suite bathroom.

"What's the holdup?" he demanded.

"It hasn't even been three minutes!" Jamie shouted back. "Keep your pants on, Cowper."

"Can I come in?" Rowan asked.

"No, you absolutely cannot!" Jamie yelled. Wincing, he sat on the edge of her bed. Needing to do something with his hands, he picked up a T-shirt from her pile of laundry. He efficiently folded it and made a new pile.

The toilet flushed, and he heard the water running, the splash of it against her hands. His heart rate increased, and his hands moved faster, folding a pair of jeans and matching socks. He glanced at his watch and saw that five minutes had passed... *Any minute now.*

If he didn't get an answer soon, he might just lose it. *Might?* He *would* lose it.

Jamie walked back into her bedroom, carrying the two small tests. Surely something that could change one's life should be bigger than that? Then again, little explosives could make big bombs.

He looked up at Jamie and jumped to his feet. "Well? Are you?"

She looked from him to the pile of folded laundry on her bed. "You folded most of my laundry? In two minutes?"

He shrugged, not bothering to explain that he'd been folding laundry since he was four or five. That in the system, he'd learned how to work fast and accurately so he didn't give people a reason to punish him. "I needed to do something. Are you pregnant?"

She handed him one stick. "I told you I was."

He looked down, saw the two blue lines and frowned. "Two lines means you are pregnant? Are you sure?"

Jamie sat down on her armchair in the corner of the room. "Very sure, Rowan. I've done more than a few pregnancy tests in my life."

He looked down at the test and shook his head. "I'm not sure how to react."

Jamie placed one leg over the other and tapped her elegant fingers against her thigh. "I can help you with that, Cowper, if you'd just let me explain."

An explanation would be good—excellent, in fact. He'd listen to anyone about anything in an effort for the world to right itself again. He hadn't felt this rattled since he'd first landed in the system.

He took a couple of deep breaths and finally nodded. "I'm listening."

Jamie played with her dress, folding the fabric as she gathered her thoughts. "We haven't talked much, and I seem to blurt out random facts in the heat of the moment. Like earlier, when I told you I was married."

He nodded. "And your husband died? How?"

"We were in a car wreck. But that's not what we're going to talk about, okay? I don't talk about the accident. Ever."

Rowan jerked at the fierce note in her voice. Right.

She sighed and when she spoke again, her tone

softened. "I seldom talk about Kaden and our marriage, but because of *that*—" she pointed at the pregnancy test he still held in his hand "—I suppose I should. But I'd appreciate it if you keep this information between us."

Whom was he going to tell? He had acquaintances, not friends. Besides, he knew the value of keeping his mouth shut. Another skill he'd learned in the system.

"I'm listening. Go on."

She looked at him as if trying to decide whether to trust him or not. He knew that nothing he could say would sway her, so he opted to remain silent and prayed she wouldn't clam up.

"Kaden and I were married for five years, and we never used contraceptives. We wanted children, and I got pregnant quite easily—that was never the problem.

"I was pregnant four times in five years, and not one of those pregnancies managed to stick. I don't believe this one will be any different," she stated. She came across as calm and effortlessly realistic. But he saw the flash of pain in her eyes before she buried it deep.

He placed his hands on the bed next to him, trying to make sense of her statement. "You miscarried every time?"

"Yeah. I've had what feels like a million tests, but they still aren't sure why I can't carry a baby to term. They call it recurrent miscarriage, or recurrent pregnancy loss, and they don't always find a reason why it happens. It's an uncommon condition."

He rubbed the back of his neck. "Shit."

Jamie laid a hand on his knee, her elegant fingers warm on his bare skin. "The thing is, whether you are mad, excited or scared, there's no point. The digital test measures hormone levels, and that three-plus sign indicates that I am more than three weeks pregnant. I got pregnant on the night we spent together."

In Jamie's eyes, he saw the truth: she *had* conceived on the night they'd spent together. Okay, then.

"Accepted?"

He nodded. Sighed. "Yeah."

"Let me explain how this works… Sometime in the next six to eight weeks, I'm going to miscarry. It's what I *do*. So there's no point in having any discussions about the baby, about the future, your role in it—anything. It's not going to happen."

He felt a hint of relief, but also, surprisingly, a hefty dose of sadness. "Are you sure about that?"

"Four times is a good clue, Cowper," Jamie told him, her tone even.

Fair point.

Jamie was handling this so much better than he was, and with a lot more class. He knew if he said that to her, she'd tell him she'd had a lot of practice, that she'd come to terms with the situation.

Anyone looking at her would think she was discussing the weather, but he'd caught a hint of devastation in her eyes, the flattening of her lips, the hunch of her shoulders. She wanted him to think she was resigned to the situation, but she wasn't.

She wanted kids; any fool could see that.

Four miscarriages and a dead husband. And an accident she wouldn't discuss. His heart ached for her.

"Did you love him? Were you happy together?"

Why was he asking, and why did he care? He was supposed to be putting distance between them, not asking about her history.

Jamie touched the bare skin on her ring finger. "We were—in the early days, at least." She touched her top lip with the tip of her tongue before continuing. "Later on, the miscarriages and our fertility issues made things harder."

As they would. "I'm so sorry."

She managed a tight smile. "Thanks." She bent over to remove her sandals, her hair falling so that her face was completely covered. "So, as I said, you don't need to worry about me and the pregnancy. It's not going anywhere."

"Does your family know about the miscarriages?" he asked.

Jamie pulled a face. "They know about the first one. We never told anyone about the others. I didn't want them to worry."

And she wanted to protect them. Just like he wanted to protect her. And there was no way he could walk out of this house, and out of her life, knowing she would miscarry his child sometime in the future. It didn't matter that there wasn't a thing he could do to change it—she was not going to do this alone. She wanted to, that much was obvious, but he was damned if he'd let her. He stood up and paced the area at the end of her bed, trying to think of an excuse to temporarily stay in her life.

But the truth was more powerful than any excuse he could concoct. "We're going to carry on seeing each other."

Jamie shot up, and the hand holding her sandal shook. "What? *Why?*"

He sent a pointed look at her stomach before his eyes reconnected with hers. "You're pregnant with my kid. You didn't get that way by yourself, so you're not doing this by yourself. For as long as that baby is around, I'm going to be around."

"There's nothing for you to do!" Jamie protested. "It's not like I can hand it over to you."

He shrugged and felt his stubborn rise. "I'm sticking and I'm staying. I am certainly not walking away and washing my hands of you and the baby."

"There will be no baby, I keep telling you that!" Jamie growled, irritation in her eyes.

"But there is *you*. And for the next few weeks, I'm going to stand at your side. I helped create this situation, and I'm sure as hell not leaving you to deal with it on your own!"

She placed a hand on her heart, her eyes glistening with emotion. "That's sweet, Rowan—"

Sweet? Ugh, what a word!

"—but silly. I'm going to go about my business as per usual and try to forget about it."

Try being the operative word. No doubt she'd be on tenterhooks for weeks. And, while he didn't consider himself particularly sensitive, he knew she was wishing this pregnancy would turn out differently—he'd seen that glimpse of hope in her eyes. When the miscarriage came, she'd be disappointed all over again.

"Despite your pragmatic approach to the situation, I suspect that waiting will be hell, and the days and weeks after your miscarriage won't be fun either. I don't bail when things get tough, so I'll be around to help distract you, and then I will be around after as well."

"It's not necess—"

"It is," he interrupted her. "It's *very* necessary. You didn't get pregnant on your own, James. And I do intend to distract you, as much as I can." He leaned back on his elbows and deliberately looked at her pillows before handing her a sexy smile. "I can think of one way…"

He'd meant it as a joke, but knew that if she so much as gave him a hint that she was up for sex, he'd have her clothes off in a flash.

Genuine humor lightened her eyes. "Funny, Cowper."

He shrugged. "It was worth a try." He stood up and held out his hand to pull her up. "Let's be friends, Jamie."

His hand swallowed hers, and he effortlessly pulled her up and into his arms. Resting his chin on her hair, he held her easily, gently.

She pulled back to look at him, her nose wrinkling. "And afterward? What then? What if we draw some lines that can't be erased? What if we cross them?"

He found it interesting, and a little scary, that her thoughts echoed his. He gathered her close again. "Let's take it day by day, sweetheart." He stroked a hand down her back before patting her butt and stepping away, which was hard to do when she was soft and fragrant and made his blood boil. "We missed out on burgers and an outdoor movie."

"Do you want to go back to Matt's place?" she asked.

It was obvious that she didn't. He took her hand and led her out of the bedroom before he gave in and pulled that lovely dress off her and laid her down on the bed. "Let's make our own movie night—right here."

In her bare feet, Jamie followed him down the hall and back into her living room. She headed into the kitchen, and the sunlight streaming in from the window turned the fabric of her dress almost transparent. He could see the outline of her legs, the gap between her thighs.

Knowing she was having his baby hadn't lessened his desire for her—not in the slightest. He still wanted her with a ferocity that astounded him. Fate kept throwing them together, tossing them into its sticky web, but he wasn't trying to break those connections, fighting to get loose.

He rather liked where he was.

And that scared him shitless.

Eight

Jamie awoke on her couch, her dress twisted around her hips, her face smothered by a particularly plump cushion. She blinked a few times, yawned and looked around her dark living room.

The detritus of their pizza-and-popcorn evening had been cleared away. Jamie cocked her head, listening for sounds coming from her kitchen. Nothing. Her house was empty. She pressed a button on her smartwatch, saw that it was close to three in the morning and wondered what time Rowan had left and why she hadn't heard him go.

Neither did she remember falling asleep...

Jamie stood up and walked over to her front door to check if it was locked—it was—and looked out the narrow pane of glass to the side, frowning when she saw Rowan's fancy car still in her drive. She saw movement in the driver's seat, and then his lights came on as the sound of the car's engine broke the silence of the muggy night.

Jamie placed her hand on the door, about to open it and wave him back inside. Why? What did she want from him?

His car backed down her driveway, and she dropped her hand from the doorknob and rested her forehead on the wooden door. Three o'clock. The time of madness and magic, indulgence and idiocy.

She couldn't—wouldn't—open her door and wave him back in. She wouldn't text him to come back.

That way madness lay...

Be sensible, Jamie. Things weren't the same as they'd been yesterday. The dynamic between them had shifted. They couldn't be fancy-free, taking what they needed from each other and walking away with a smile and a wave.

She was pregnant with his baby...

A baby she would lose.

Jamie turned, placed her back against the door and slowly sank to the floor. She rested her cheek on her bent knee and forced herself to think.

They weren't lovers, and they weren't—despite Rowan's lovely suggestion—friends. Or not yet, anyway.

The thing was, friendship required trust and openness, traits neither of them possessed. He wasn't a talker. She knew very little about his past.

That he'd grown up in foster care was all she'd gleaned from him. She recognized his reticence, his inability to open up, because she was the same. Her heart had spun locks and chains around itself when Kaden died, trapping all her memories. She could talk to anyone on a vast range of subjects, but sharing her innermost thoughts was utterly impossible.

How could she tell the people who loved her husband like a son, like a brother, that she and Kaden had mentioned divorce just before he died? That they'd wanted different things and could no longer find any common ground? That sometimes love wasn't enough?

Funny... The one person who would understand, or who would at least not judge her, was Rowan. Although he'd never been married, he seemed to understand people. Jamie thought he'd understand how love could become distorted, how lost a person could feel in what once had been a fairy-tale marriage.

She also suspected he'd know how it felt to live with guilt and regret.

She appreciated his offer to stand by her, respected the fact that he wasn't bailing, but a part of her wished he'd leave her to navigate the next few weeks on her own. If he did that, she could try and forget that she was pregnant—she rarely had any pregnancy symptoms except for changes in her taste and tiredness—and concentrate on her business, on living her life as normally as possible.

She didn't want to become used to having him in

her life, relying on him for emotional support. She was used to living her life solo, with no emotional attachments. She liked it that way.

But Rowan was determined to see her through this, to support her and be with her—though what he could do, she had no idea. She appreciated the sentiment. She did. But, God, every time she looked at him, she'd remember that inside her was a jumble of his DNA and hers, trying to grow, trying to survive.

A baby she couldn't allow herself to want. A child she'd ultimately lose.

Jamie rested the back of her head on the door and looked up at the dark ceiling of her hallway. Why was this happening to her? Was life punishing her?

At the beginning of her marriage, she'd been desperate for a child and had started collecting clothes and all the paraphernalia a baby required. She'd been sad when she lost her first baby, but figured number two would be healthy. After that second loss, she'd struggled to stay upbeat and tempered her excitement when she heard she was pregnant with baby number three. After *that* miscarriage, she'd told Kaden she was done, but he'd begged her to try again. She did, and the only person who'd been surprised by that loss was Kaden.

He was furious when she donated all the baby clothes and equipment, devastated when she told him that she couldn't do it again.

One argument rolled into another, which rolled

into another. Misery moved into their home and lives, settled down and took root.

The headlights of a car shining through the glass side panel jerked her out of her reverie, and she climbed to her feet, feeling emotionally exhausted.

She could work fifteen-hour days for weeks on end without feeling tired, but people and the emotions they raised exhausted her.

It was so much easier being alone, keeping one's distance.

As she climbed the steps to her bedroom, she remembered making love to Rowan. While being alone was easier, it certainly wasn't as much fun.

Jamie stood on her parents' front porch, waving at the car reversing down the driveway. By her calculation, that was the last of her parents' party guests, thank God. When she arranged for Rowan to be her date, she'd expected a fun and flirty evening, a little dancing, a little necking. He was a guy she liked, someone she wanted to have an affair with. A scant week later, she was the woman who was carrying his child.

They'd crossed the line from fun and flirty to sedate and serious. *Blergh.*

Her childhood home had been full-to-bursting for most of the night, and she'd taken on the role of host so her mom could enjoy her evening as the guest of honor. As a result, Jamie had barely seen Rowan. In fact, she didn't even know whether he'd gone home or not.

She'd caught glimpses of him throughout the evening, either talking to Greg or Chas or, surprisingly, her grandmother. She remembered him bringing bottles of champagne from the kitchen and helping out behind the bar when the bartender had seemed overwhelmed. He didn't make a fuss or bring attention to himself; he was simply there, doing what was needed when it was needed.

Despite knowing only her and Greg, he didn't try and monopolize her, seeming to understand that she was busy and couldn't give him any of her attention. A few times, he did suggest she take a break; and when she didn't, he handed her a soft drink or a plate of food she could eat on the go. He'd looked after her, but so subtly she'd barely noticed him doing it.

Sneaky. And sweet.

Suddenly exhausted, Jamie sat down on the front-porch swing, kicked off her shoes and tucked her heels under her butt. She put a cushion behind her head and considered taking a ten-minute nap—just long enough to revive her so she could make the drive home.

If Rowan were still here, she'd ask him to take her. And if he came inside with her, there was a good chance she'd jump him.

And really, who could blame her? He was hot, sexy, ripped and an incredible lover. He knew how to touch her, how to make her writhe and whimper. He seemed to instinctively know whether she needed to slow down or speed up, how to touch her, where and when to kiss her. He knew *her*…

"There you are."

Jamie turned to see him standing just outside the front door, hands in the pockets of his suit pants. He'd discarded his jacket and tie and rolled up the sleeves of his shirt, revealing his strong forearms.

"Hey. I was just thinking about you," Jamie said, patting the cushion beside her. Since she couldn't tell him about her take-me-against-a-wall fantasy, she uttered a white lie. "I didn't know if you'd left already."

"Without letting you know?" Rowan asked, sitting down next to her and resting his hand on her knee. "I thought you might need me to drive you home. You look exhausted."

Because she could, she rested her temple on Rowan's big shoulder. "Yeah, I'm pretty shattered. But I think my parents had a nice time."

"They did. Your folks told me to tell you how grateful they are for your help and that they love you. Oh, and that they were going up to bed."

"Thanks. What's Gran up to?" Jamie asked, placing her hand on top of his and linking their fingers.

"She's drinking whiskey and playing poker with Greg and Chas," Rowan told her.

Jamie released a small groan. "Gran will drink them under the table, clean out their pockets and still be awake at sunrise. They, on the other hand, will wake up with a helluva hangover."

Rowan's low laugh rumbled over her skin. "Your gran is quite a character."

"That she is," Jamie agreed. She lifted her head to look at his shadowed face. "I hope my mom didn't ask you too many questions?"

Rowan took a while to answer her. "She cornered me shortly after dinner and asked me to provide her with three character references, told me she was going to get a cop friend of hers to do a background check on me and demanded a copy of my bank statements."

Jamie stared at him. Her mother was overprotective of her—they all were—but those requests were bordering on the ridiculous. "I'm so sorry, Row. It's just that I've never brought anyone home, so she's adding three and four and getting… Oh!"

She narrowed her eyes at his smirk, and when it turned into one of his rare smiles, she punched his shoulder, an action he barely noticed. "You jerk! I thought you were being serious!"

"Who says I'm not?" Rowan asked.

"The crinkling of your eyes and the dimple in your cheek," Jamie told him, unable to hold back her own grin. "What did she really say to you?"

"She welcomed me, told me she was happy to meet me and asked me what I did, how long I've lived in the city. Normal getting-to-know-you conversation."

Jamie handed him a suspicious look. "I'm more inclined to believe your earlier nonsense than that load of hooey. What's the truth?"

His mouth twitched. "She wanted to know how long we'd been seeing each other and whether it was serious."

That sounded more like her mom. "What did you tell her?"

Rowan surprised her by turning his head and kissing her forehead. "That we're still getting to know each other and are taking things slowly."

"Good answer."

"I'm glad you approve," Rowan told her, laughter in his voice. "I liked her. Mostly because there's no doubt that she'd move heaven and earth for you. She adores you."

Jamie nodded, tears burning her eyes. "She does. I've never doubted how much I was loved." She heard her words and wished she could yank them back. She grimaced. "I'm so sorry, Row. That was inconsiderate."

"You don't need to apologize to me for having a great family, Jamie. I'm happy you do." He turned, lifted his arm and rested it on the back cushion, his fingers playing with her hair. "You look very pretty tonight. Did I tell you that?"

She knew he was trying to change the subject, and she felt a little sad that he wouldn't let her in. Then again, if he started pushing her about Kaden and the accident, would she be brave enough to open up and tell him how she blamed herself for the events of that day? How was it that this man—so emotionally detached, himself—was the one with whom she felt tempted to share her secrets?

Also, not sleeping with him, *being friends*, was killing her. She appreciated him not running from her and this pregnancy, but she'd appreciate him far more if he took her to bed. Yes, the mental and emotional connection she felt for him terrified her—she risked feeling a lot more for him than she should. But her desire for him swamped her common sense.

Maybe it was hormones, maybe he'd cast some sort of spell on her, but she needed to make love to him again. Immediately.

Rowan wrapped a strand of her hair around his finger and watched it slide off. "You have the softest hair I've ever touched." He lifted his gaze, and his eyes, deep and dark, slammed into hers. "And the most kissable mouth."

"Do I?" Jamie asked softly, feeling that warm wave of desire and need rising inside her.

"You know you do," Rowan told her, bending his head so that his lips hovered over hers. "Can I kiss you, James?"

"God, I wish you would!"

He laughed at her heartfelt response, and Jamie felt the little puffs of air on her lips. Sick of waiting, she lifted her mouth to touch his and sighed when they finally connected.

Lips locked and tongues tangled and teeth scraped, and she loved it all, every second of it. There was something magical about being kissed by a man who knew what he was doing, whose sole purpose was to give you pleasure. Jamie moaned deep in her throat, and Rowan deepened the kiss, turning it more demanding.

Minutes passed, and Jamie gave herself up to the moment, relishing being the object of Rowan's passion. When he picked her up and laid her across his lap, she leaned back against his strong arm and whimpered when his hand came up to cover her breast, his thumb gliding over her nipple. She wanted him. Here, in the dark shadows on her parents' porch while her gran and brothers played poker behind the living room window.

"Shhh," Rowan whispered. "We've got to be super-quiet or else your dad will be out here with a shotgun."

"He doesn't own a shotgun, but he does have a high-powered bow," she told him, grinning.

"Either way, I'd prefer not to be shot, by neither bullet nor arrow," Rowan said quietly, his white teeth glinting in the darkness.

As much as she wanted to make love to Rowan, they couldn't do it out here, in the open. "Take me home, Row, and let's do this properly."

"I don't know if that's a good idea," Rowan muttered. He pulled back to look at her, his brows pulling together in a small frown. "James, I'm trying to be supportive, to—"

"But you have been," she interrupted him. "Instead of ghosting me, you're here, helping as we wait for the inevitable to happen." She hesitated and then shrugged. What harm could it do? He could only say no. "I still want to have a fling with you,

Rowan, and we might as well have some fun while we wait. Baby or no baby, I'm still not asking for anything more than sex."

She honestly thought he'd turn her down again and was surprised when he nodded. "Okay."

"You're agreeing?" Jamie clarified.

"I was an idiot the first time I refused and regretted it the moment you walked out my door. I've wanted you every moment since; and since I believe that you are a strong, capable woman who knows what she's doing and what she wants, I'm not going to say no again."

Yay. And thank God. "Great. So are you going to take me home now?"

Rowan's mouth kicked up into a sexy smile. "Eventually." His hand slid under her dress and stroked the length of her outer thigh. "Let's do this first." Before she could finish that thought, Rowan covered her mouth with his and slipped his hand between her thighs, stroking her with unerring accuracy.

He pulled aside her panties, and then his fingers were on her bare folds, finding her nub and stroking it delicately, building her pleasure stroke by stroke. He pulled back to look into her eyes, his expression super-serious. "You are so incredibly beautiful, Jamie."

She tried to smile, wished she could, but all her concentration was on what he was doing below, hoping he'd slide his fingers inside her. As if he'd heard her, Rowan pushed one finger into her, then another; and Jamie sighed, her head falling back, lost in the moment. His thumb swiped her clitoris, and she pushed her hips up, wanting more.

"I wish you were inside me," she told him, her whisper sounding needy. She could feel his erection, steel-hard against her hip, and while his fingers were great, she wanted him to come on the ride with her.

"Later. Tonight, this is about you," Rowan told her, widening his fingers a little and tapping her inside channel. Jamie placed her fist in her mouth to keep her whimpers back and felt tears burn her eyes. She looked up into his masculine face, and her eyes clashed with his, filled with a dark blue fire.

He pushed deeper inside and rocked his hand. She felt herself peak, then fly on angel wings toward the sun. He didn't stop stroking her, wringing every drop of pleasure from her, and when she could think again, she couldn't remember ever having a rolling series of orgasms from one man's hand before.

When she was finally done, she slumped against Rowan's chest and tried to regulate her harsh breathing, feeling completely wrung out. Rowan rearranged her clothing, dropped a kiss in her hair. She should thank him, and she would—in a minute. When she remembered how to speak.

She yawned, curled up and rested her hand on his chest. She was so tired, but it would be rude to fall asleep...

Nine

"Seriously, what the hell were you thinking, tucking into Gran's homemade whiskey last night?"

Jamie scowled at Greg, then at Chas, though neither her brother nor brother-in-law noticed because they both had their heads in their hands, thoroughly hungover.

When she'd driven back to her parents' house earlier that morning, she found Greg and Chas passed out on the leather couches in the living room. She'd run up the stairs to the guest bedroom, peeked inside and found Rowan's clothes piled up on the bed and the shower running. He was alive—no thanks to her brother, brother-in-law or grandmother. Thank God, because she still had plans for him.

Jamie winced, feeling remorseful. After their

conversation about sex, she'd allowed Rowan to pleasure her and then she'd passed out. She didn't believe in owing anyone anything when it came to sex, but Rowan deserved some of her undivided attention.

As soon as he came down, she'd take him home and do exactly that.

"We were feeling brave," Chas protested weakly, raising his pale green face.

Jamie rolled her eyes.

"And when did you start drinking tequila?" Jamie demanded, remembering the bottle on the coffee table and the dirty shot glasses.

Greg raised his head, squinting. "Uh, that was Gran's idea. Said she wasn't sleepy and wanted something with a kick."

Jamie covered her face with her hands. "Oh, God."

Chas frowned. "I think Rowan proposed to her at some stage. She said yes. So that's official."

Oh, dear Lord.

Jamie pushed her sunglasses up into her hair and rubbed her eyes with her thumb and index finger. While she could remember their hot and wild interaction on the porch in great detail, she didn't recall Rowan picking her up and carrying her up the stairs to the guest bedroom. When she woke, somewhere around five, her dress was lying over the back of a chair, and a light throw covered her from her chest to her toes. Her bag sat on the bedside table, next to a glass of water. She'd debated going back to sleep but decided she should find out whether Rowan was still in the house or if he'd left to go back to his place.

So she'd dressed and tiptoed down the stairs to find carnage, with Rowan curled up in a too-small chair next to her sleeping brothers. Wide awake then, she tidied up a little before deciding to head home for a shower and a change of clothes.

Because Greg had parked her in, she drove Rowan's car back to her place and returned here to find a still-quiet house. A note in the kitchen told her that her mom had gone out for an early breakfast with her friends and that her father had left for a round of golf. It was Jamie's job to revive and restore her brothers and her man.

Her *man*.

Jamie placed her linked hands on her stomach and pushed them into her sternum, trying to hold back the wave of grief that threatened to cut her legs out from under her. Kaden had been her man—the man she'd married, the one she'd adored. From the moment she'd met him, she knew he'd be the man she'd marry. He'd felt the same. Neither of them had expected the troubles that followed, and she'd never envisioned coming to a place where divorce was an option. Would she ever be able to let go of the guilt, forgive herself and move on? Would she ever be able to love Row—another man—again?

Jamie scrubbed her hands over her face, memories of Kaden bombarding her. How many times had they eaten breakfast on this deck, him kicking back in jeans and a T-shirt, sunglasses over his face? He'd played football with the Bacall men on the wide swathe of lawn that was her dad's pride and joy, practiced his putting on her dad's mini green at the end of the garden. Having a sporty father and brother, Kaden had fit right in. The men in her family played tennis and golf, went to ball games, watched games together. Losing Kaden dropped her family to their knees.

Rowan was very, very different from her red-haired, dark-eyed husband, and not just in looks. Kaden, like her, had been a child of privilege, but Rowan had a toughness about him. His eyes told anyone who cared to look that this man had lived a million lives, not all of them good. Kaden had held a couple of degrees, was bright as hell, and after leaving college, immediately stepped into a job at Bacall Media.

Rowan was wealthy—ridiculously so—but he was a self-made man, and he'd pulled himself up by his bootstraps. Everything he had, he'd worked for himself, and Jamie admired his guts and his perseverance. It took a special type of courage to come out on top when the odds were stacked against you.

"Gran and Rowan are engaged, by the way," Chas muttered, less green now but still pale.

Jamie smiled at him repeating himself. "Really? When did this happen?"

Chas rubbed his forehead. "I think I recall her stroking his biceps—which, I have to admit, are pretty fine—and her telling him that if you didn't want him, she'd take him. That he'd make beautiful babies."

"He told her that he'd marry her tomorrow," Greg added.

"Who's getting married?"

Three heads shot up. Upon seeing Rowan, both Chas and Greg groaned. Jamie understood why; Rowan looked as fresh as he did when he'd first arrived at the party last night. Sure, his clothes were a bit wrinkled, but he'd finger-combed his wet hair, and his eyes looked remarkably clear.

"If you're going to look all *GQ* gorgeous, then go away," Greg told him, waving a listless hand.

Rowan stopped by Jamie's chair, dropped a kiss on the top of her head and murmured, "Good morning." He pulled out a chair, sat down and reached for the jug of orange juice and a glass. He grinned at her brothers. "Feeling rough, boys?"

Greg and Chas both glared at him. "Are you human?" Greg demanded.

Rowan lifted his big shoulders. "I never suffer from hangovers. I drink, sleep for a few hours and wake up feeling normal."

"That isn't right. Or fair," Greg whined. "I feel like a couple of lumberjacks are using a chain saw to fell a sequoia in my head, and my mouth tastes like a landfill."

"Lovely," Jamie murmured.

Rowan turned to face her, remorse in his eyes. "I'm so sorry about last night."

His apology was sincere, but there was embarrassment in his eyes. He was properly ashamed, and Jamie found herself placing her hand on his bare arm and squeezing. "Relax. Gran's brand of whiskey is industrial strength, and it's felled many a man before you."

Rowan winced. "I believe you because normally I can hold my liquor and it takes a lot to make me drunk. And a lot more to make me fall asleep in a chair." He rubbed the back of his neck and looked at Jamie. "You've changed. Have you been out?"

She nodded. "I drove back to my place."

"How?" Concern flickered in his eyes. "Greg parked you in last night. Did you take his car?"

Seeing Rowan's fancy sports car in the driveway was a temptation she'd been unable to resist. "No, I borrowed yours. I didn't think you'd mind."

"You drove my Aston Martin DB11?" Rowan asked, sounding like he was choking. God, he made it sound like she'd attempted to pilot a jet fighter. It was super-powerful, sure, but still just a car.

Jamie, irritated by his lack of faith, decided to mess with him a little. "Is it supposed to make such a terrible noise when you change gears?"

She hid her smile at the three groans, and Rowan scrunched up his face, obviously in pain. "And I'm sure it won't cost much to fix the scrape on its side panel," she added, trying to look insouciant before pulling a "whoops!" expression onto her face.

Rowan gripped the arms of his chair, and Chas and Greg looked like she'd stolen their will to live. God, how stupid did they think she was? And what was it about men that made them lose their ability to think rationally when cars were mentioned?

"Chill, guys. I'm joking. The car is perfectly fine."

Three expressions lightened, and Rowan's shoulders dropped half a foot. He shook his head and laid a hand on his heart. "You took about ten years off my life. That car is my baby, and it usually spends its life in a garage."

Jamie flashed him an impertinent grin. "Next time, don't assume I can't drive a powerful car with a stick."

He winced. "My bad. I seem to be racking them up this morning." He looked around, frowning. "Speaking of, where are your parents? I should apologize."

Jamie shook her head. "Dad is golfing and Mom is out with some friends. And there's nothing to apologize for. You fell asleep. Big deal."

"But you might like to find our grandmother and start making arrangements," Greg told him, his arm casually draped around Chas's shoulders.

Rowan frowned at them. "What arrangements?"

Chas grinned. "Apparently you agreed to marry her last night."

Rowan grimaced. "Oh, Jesus. Seriously?"

"Seriously," Greg nodded. "She's enamored with your Thor-like body."

"Aren't we all," Chas said, then sighed. When Greg growled and play-punched his shoulder, Chas laughed. "Oh, please, we've both got eyes in our heads."

To Jamie's amusement and relief, Rowan simply laughed. "Show some respect, boys. I'm going to be your grandfather-in-law."

Greg and Chas laughed, and Jamie grinned at Rowan, delighted. Delighted because he was so unfazed by her brothers, because he had a sense of humor and also because he looked so damn fine sitting next to her on her parents' deck.

Like he belonged there.

Her heart dropped to her feet, and her mood plummeted as well. He *couldn't* and he *didn't*. The only person who should be sitting there was Kaden, and he was dead. She'd watched him die, and she hadn't been able to save him. It was her fault he was gone; her fault that Rowan was sitting in his chair today, next to her, chatting with her brother and his husband as if he'd always been part of their lives.

Nobody could take Kaden's place. She wouldn't let that happen. Ever.

Jamie launched herself to her feet, pushing her chair back so hard that it scraped against the stone tiles. Her eyes fell on Rowan's surprised face. "I need to go. We should go," she muttered, cursing her burning eyes.

Rowan followed her. She couldn't look at Greg or Chas, knowing that she'd see sympathy on their faces. They might've worked out why she was so spooked.

A small frown pulled Rowan's eyebrows together. "Is something wrong?" he asked.

It was the gentleness in his voice that got to her, the tenderness in his eyes. She couldn't cope with either, just like she couldn't cope with the way she'd reacted to his touch last night, how she lost and found herself in his arms, how his deep voice caused her stomach to flip over, her heart to bounce off her rib cage.

And, intellectually, she knew it wasn't Rowan's fault that her family liked him, that they hoped she was moving on. She didn't want to move on. She liked her life the way it was: safe and stable. Since stepping into that elevator with Rowan, her life had been a roller coaster. Kisses, sex, back and forth, outside orgasms and, let's not forget, a very unwelcome pregnancy.

It was too much for her to handle.

She also couldn't bear the thought of loving and losing someone again. She couldn't bear to be happy again, feeling connected and complete, and then losing the person who made her feel that way. It hurt too damn much. She never wanted to experience that again.

Ever.

Rowan slowly nodded. "Let me see you to your car, James."

His instinctual understanding that she was suddenly in a dark place nearly dropped her to her knees.

Rowan followed Jamie home and pulled in behind her in the driveway to her vintage gray-blue house. He exited his car, and while he waited for her to do the same, he cast an eye over her property.

He'd been so freaked out the last time he was here, he hadn't taken in many details.

Or any at all.

But, having done a restoration of a similar house, he knew it was probably a three-bedroom, two-bath, with hardwood floors and a wood-burning fireplace in the living room. The house was completely fenced in, had great curb appeal and was perfectly positioned, being close to parks, shops, excellent restaurants and a train station.

He approved. Not that she wanted or needed his approval.

Rowan stared down at his shoes, remembering her sudden change of mood, the tears glittering in her copper-colored eyes. One minute, she'd been laughing and teasing him; the next, she'd looked like he'd kicked her favorite kitten. Back at her folks' house, it felt like she'd disappeared into herself, too far for him to reach her. A thought, a memory, *something* had instantaneously sucked the life and joy out of her. He wanted to know what it was. He wanted to know *her*.

God.

He rubbed a hand down his face. He was wading into quicksand and was rapidly sinking. Accompanying her to her parents' party should've been a polite in and out, no harm done. But instead of snobby rich people, he'd found a warm, loving family who teased and laughed, happy to be in each other's company. It was obvious that Jamie's parents adored her, as did her brother and his husband, but they all worried about her, judging by the concerned looks they sent her way when she wasn't looking.

And they'd been ridiculously over-the-top happy that he'd come as Jamie's partner. He'd caught that in the way her father gripped his shoulder when they shook hands, the way her mom looked at him, gratitude in her eyes.

Rowan felt like he was part of a story they'd all read and he hadn't.

He liked the Bacalls and he liked Jamie too. He loved the way she rolled her amazing eyes, the way she pursed her lips when she was trying not to laugh. He even liked the way she teased him— she'd had him going about his car!—and the fact that she wasn't scared to do so. He loved the fact that she offered her opinions easily and openly, not particularly caring whether her family agreed or not. He liked her sharp mind, lusted over her sensational body.

Adored the way she fell apart under his touch.

Yeah, he was skidding down the feel-more-than-I-should hill, and if he didn't change course, he would end up flying off a cliff.

He watched her open the door to her car, looking anywhere but at him. With her hair pulled into a high ponytail and wearing a cropped T-shirt and old jeans, she looked more like a college student than a successful business owner. She most certainly didn't look pregnant.

"How are you?" he demanded, realizing he hadn't asked after her today. He gestured to her stomach. "How are you feeling? Anything I should know about?"

She shook her head. "It's still too early. It normally happens between ten and eleven weeks."

He thought about his schedule and remembered that he was due to fly to Nashville around that time for a meeting with Matt, who'd temporarily relocated to oversee a shopping mall development. Nashville was a two-hour flight; he could be back quite quickly if Jamie needed him.

But he suspected she wouldn't. Jamie didn't want to rely on anyone, anytime. He wanted her to rely on him, though, to look to him for comfort and support. To be her primary connection. *Jesus, Cowper.* He lived his life solo. He didn't *do* connections...

What the hell? This wasn't who he was, what he wanted, how he lived his life. He didn't get this involved with anyone—ever.

Jamie gestured to her house. "I'm going in. I have chores to do, and then I'm going to take a nap."

Despite his mind and emotions being at war, Rowan didn't want to leave her. "Do you need a hand?"

Jamie's eyebrows flew up. "To do my laundry and clean my bathroom?"

He shrugged. He'd done a lot worse. "I thought you might like some company, and I don't mind pitching in."

She blew out a long stream of air and shook her head. "I'm grumpy and sad and irritable, and I think I need some time alone, Row."

Fair enough. Stepping up to her, Rowan put his hands on her hips. When she tensed, he shook his head. "Shhh. Just hang on, okay?"

He wrapped his arms around her, holding her close. Slowly, like a leaky balloon, the tautness left her body, and the hands she'd kept at her sides lifted to his waist, then inched around his back to fist in his shirt. She laid her head on his chest, and he, somehow, knew that her eyes were closed and that she was fighting the urge to cry.

He wanted to know why she felt so unhinged, what was going on behind her lovely facade. But he couldn't push—wouldn't. He respected emotional barriers and knew that it was a deeply personal and hard choice to allow anyone behind the wall. He wouldn't bulldoze his way through.

After a few minutes, he loosened his hold and kissed her temple before stepping back. "Call me if you need me. As you know, I can fold laundry."

She nodded, managing a small smile. "If your current career doesn't work out, it's something you can explore."

He touched her cheek with his knuckle. "Bye, sweetheart. Get some sleep, okay?"

Jamie walked up to her front door, and he watched until she was inside. Then he scrubbed his hands over his face.

Yep, flying off that cliff wouldn't hurt, but the landing could kill him.

Ten

I can't make dinner on Friday, sorry. Will reschedule ASAP.

Jamie reread the message from Rowan, frowned and laid her phone on her desk. Just yesterday, he'd called to confirm the invitation for them to join Greg and Chas for dinner Friday evening. He'd offered to collect her from her place at seven and drive them all to the world-famous restaurant a half hour out of town.

She'd never been to Ruby Red and had been looking forward to the gastronomic experience. It was also one of Rowan's favorite restaurants, and he'd told her he was always happy to eat there. So why had he canceled?

She didn't know him well, but she knew he wasn't one to change his mind without a good reason. And why hadn't he called her to explain instead of sending her a terse text? That wasn't like him either.

Jamie leaned back in her office chair and stared at the painting on the wall opposite her. She hadn't seen Rowan since he'd hugged her on her driveway a week ago. He'd given her space and, after a few days, called to check on her. Since then, they'd spoken a few times and texted often. He'd told her he was looking forward to seeing her Friday night and, yeah, she was longing to see him too. Preferably naked. This affair she was trying to have with him was taking a hell of a long time to manifest.

She picked up her phone and scrolled through her contacts, looking for his number. She hit the green button when she found it—and was surprised when a brisk female voice answered. "Mr. Cowper's phone. How can I help you?"

"Uh... I was looking for Rowan. Is he around? It's Jamie speaking."

"Mr. Cowper is currently unavailable. Can I take a message?"

Jamie was about to ask that he return her call when she heard the distinctive sound of a doctor being called on an intercom system.

"Would you mind telling me where, exactly, Rowan is right now?"

"At McKinley Hospital. He should be resting, but he's been glued to his phone."

Jamie's heart jumped into her throat. "He's in the hospital? What the hell for?"

"Uh… I can't tell you that. Jeez, I shouldn't have told you he is here. And now he wants his phone… Hold on."

"Cowper."

His voice sounded croaky but strong, and some of her panic receded. If he was talking and sounding tense, he wasn't at death's door. "Rowan? Why are you in the hospital? What's the matter? Are you okay?"

It was Thursday and she'd spoken to him four times this week already. Not once had he mentioned that he was going into the hospital. Or had his visit there been unexpected?

"Did you have a heart attack? An allergic reaction? What's wrong with you?" she demanded, hearing the hint of terror in her voice, tasting it on her tongue.

"A heart attack, James? No, I tripped while running and fell on my wrist, fracturing it. It needed a pin, so I had surgery."

"Oh." God, he sounded so calm. "Are you okay? Is it sore? Are you in pain?"

"They gave me something. It's in a cast. I feel a bit spacey from the anesthetic."

"They put you under?"

"Yeah, they don't like their patients wriggling

while they put steel pins in their limbs," Rowan replied, and she heard the amusement in his voice.

"Can I do anything? Bring you anything?" Jamie asked, hoping he'd say yes so she'd have an excuse to fly down there to check if he was okay.

"No, I'm good…"

Rowan's voice faded out, and Jamie heard the distinct sounds of a low argument before the Irish-accented nurse spoke again.

"Mr. Cowper could do with a change of clothing and a lift home. I am not happy about him taking a taxi in his current state."

Jamie heard Rowan growl "I'm fine!" in the background.

"He vomited after surgery, and he's still a little shaky. Some people react badly to a general anesthetic, and he's one of them."

"Will you give me back my phone, Nurse?"

"Are you coming?" the nurse asked Jamie.

"I'm coming," Jamie confirmed. "I'll be there as soon as I can. Don't let him bully you."

"Ha! As if…"

Jamie asked to speak to Rowan again, and before he could argue—and she knew she would—she spoke quickly. "I'm going to your office. Tell your PA to let me up to your apartment."

"Look, it's not necessary. I'll get a taxi, make my way home."

Wow. He really didn't want her to help him. Too bad he was going to get a solid dose of exactly that. "I'll be there as soon as I can."

"Jamie, I'm good!"

"Shut up, Cowper," Jamie gently told him before disconnecting the call. Two minutes later, she was out the door.

Jamie walked into McKinley Hospital forty-five minutes later, holding a small bag containing a change of clothes for Rowan. She stepped into the elevator, thinking about Rowan and his very minimalistic apartment.

She hadn't been back to his place since the night they'd first made love. At the time, she'd had him on her mind and hadn't paid attention to his decor. Walking around on her own, she realized that his place was huge, hardly contained any furniture, and was stark and cold. With its undecorated white walls and modern furniture, it reminded her of a dormitory or institution. He had no art on display, no photographs, nothing personal. In fact, for a stupidly wealthy guy, his apartment contained little in the way of worldly possessions. There was the requisite flat-screen and a huge stereo system, but that was it.

She wondered why such a wealthy guy in his thirties had so little, apart from his two fancy cars, in the way of personal possessions. Why did Rowan live in a place that reminded her of a walk-in fridge?

Jamie stepped out of the elevator and walked toward the nurses' station. A tall nurse stood nearby, holding a tablet. She raised her eyebrows at Jamie's approach. The name tag fixed to her ship's-prow bosom stated her name was Briggs.

"I'm here to see Rowan Cowper," Jamie told her, showing her his bag.

She nodded. "Three doors down, room six."

Jamie found the door to room six, tapped on it and poked her head inside. Rowan turned to look and gestured for her to come in.

His face held a faint greenish tinge, and his right wrist lay on his lap, encased in a cast from the bottom of his fingers to his elbow.

"How are you feeling? How's the—you hurt your head as well?" she asked, seeing the trail of four stitches running across his forehead. "Holy crap, Rowan! What the hell did you do?"

He pulled a face, looking embarrassed. "I was running and I tripped. Over what, I don't know. I landed on my wrist and cracked my head on the side of a wooden flower box."

She touched his shoulder, needing to connect, to reassure herself. She swallowed, blinked back her tears and pushed away thoughts of what could've happened. She lifted the gym bag she'd found in the cupboard of his all-white bedroom. "I brought you a change of clothes if you want to shower."

He grimaced. "That was the scary nurse's idea. I'd rather sort myself out at home."

One-handed? She didn't think so. But, yes, she understood why he'd prefer to be at home. Even if his place very much resembled this hospital room. "Okay, I hear you."

"Thank God someone does," Rowan muttered.

"Having a hard time controlling the world, Cowper?"

He narrowed his eyes at her, and Jamie laughed. She picked up his bag, dumped it on the bed, opened the zipper and pulled out shorts and a linen button-down shirt. "Need some help?"

"I've got it," Rowan told her.

Jamie sat on the visitor's chair and watched him struggle to take the hospital gown off his head with one hand. She heard a couple of creative curses, and when his face drained of even more color and he bit his lip, obviously in pain, she stood up. "Ready to ask for some help yet?"

Rowan glared at her, the effect dimmed by the pain in his eyes. Ignoring his scowl, Jamie eased his hospital gown off, pulled the fabric down his arm and tossed it onto the chair. She wrinkled her nose at the blood on his chest and allowed herself the pleasure of looking at all that warm skin across his fantastically ridged stomach.

"I like it when you look at me like that," Rowan murmured. Jamie's eyes slammed into his, and she caught her breath at the passion in his gaze, the slight quirk at the corner of his mouth. "I have a raging headache and my wrist is on fire but God, I still want you more than I need to breathe. Or a pain pill."

"Then why haven't you been around?" Jamie asked.

"I thought you needed some space," he replied.

"It's been hell staying away from you," he added, his tone serious.

She sent him a glance, and the serious look in his eyes had her sucking in her breath. Because she wasn't sure what to say or how to react, she opted for humor. "Exactly how hard did you hit your head, Cowper?"

"Do you always do that?"

"Do what?" she asked, nodding for him to put his good arm into the sleeve.

Rowan shoved his arm into the fabric, and Jamie pulled the shirt around his shoulders. "Make a joke when things get serious?"

She forced herself to look him in the eye. "But we aren't getting serious, Rowan. Neither of us does serious, remember?"

Looking frustrated, he pushed his hand into his hair, yelping when his fingers connected with his stitched-up cut. "Ow, shit! Dammit!"

Rowan looked down at the sleeve she was holding, and she shook her head at her stupidity. "I'm a crap nurse." She pulled his shirt off and started again, threading his cast-covered wrist through the sleeve before efficiently pulling on his shirt.

"I can do this, you know."

"Well, I'd like to get back to work before sundown," Jamie retorted.

"I didn't ask you to come down here," Rowan muttered.

True enough. Jamie cocked her head to the side as she did up his buttons. "Wow. You really are uncomfortable with someone helping you. Why is that?"

He shrugged. "It's easier. When you've never had anyone to rely on, you quickly get used to sorting yourself out."

"Nobody? Ever?"

Rowan opened his mouth to speak, snapped it closed and reached for the shorts lying next to his bag. He pulled them out of her hands. "I can manage these."

He probably could. Or, judging by the light of battle in his eyes, he would die trying. "Go for it."

He pushed back the covers of the bed, and she took a moment to admire the way his black briefs outlined his impressive package. *Not the time, Bacall!* He swung his long, muscular legs out of bed and dropped his feet to the floor. Lowering the shorts, he maneuvered one foot through the fabric, then the other, and pulled the garment up to his hips using one hand. Jamie deliberately looked at her watch, then at the ceiling, then at her watch again.

"Smart-ass," Rowan mumbled.

"Stubborn," she shot back. She placed her fists on her hips, tipping her head back to look at him. Even battered, he looked super-sexy. "How are you going to drive? Type? Work?"

"One-handed," Rowan replied.

"You can't do everything one-handed, Cowper."

"Why? Are you offering to move in?" Rowan asked, reaching inside his bag to pull out a pair of flip-flops.

She matched his challenging stare with one of her own. "I would if you needed me to."

Rowan held her eye, his turning stormy. "Just like you, I don't need anyone."

Yeah, got it. Message received. Jamie held up her hands and backed away from the bed. "I think my work here is done."

She picked her bag off the back of the visitor's chair, hoping he couldn't see how hurt she was. She got it: he was a loner, independent as hell, but she *had* left her office and her busy workday to get him clothes, to help him out. She didn't need his undying gratitude, but a thank-you would be nice. And really, she had whiplash trying to keep up with his contradictory messages. He wanted to sleep with her—*desperately* —yet he couldn't bear for her to help him?

He made her head spin—this time, not in a good way—but she wasn't going to force her help on him. The guy could take a hundred years to get things done, if he got them done at all.

His choice.

Jamie hoisted her bag up onto her shoulder, spun around and headed for the door, her back straight and her head up high. Inconsiderate jerk! She'd rushed down here to help him, as any friend would do...

Friend. She stopped abruptly. When she'd told him she was pregnant, he'd told her he wanted to see her through the next few weeks, that he wanted to be her friend. But when things went wrong for him, she couldn't be his?

There was something very wrong with this logic.

She turned around, dropped her bag onto the bed and shook her head. "Stop being a dick, Cowper. You might feel uncomfortable asking for help, taking help, but suck it up. If you can take me to dinner—a double date with my brother and his husband—or get me off on my mother's porch, be there for me as this pregnancy progresses, then you can accept my help too.

"I am going to drive you back to your morgue-like home, help you rinse the blood from your disgusting hair and help you out." She leaned down, swiped her mouth across his and saw his eyes widen in surprise. She pulled back and looked around. "Where are your clothes? The ones you came in with?"

His sigh suggested defeat, and he gestured to the bedside cabinet. "What's wrong with my place?"

"Too sterile, too boring, too white," Jamie told him, pulling out his blood-splattered sneakers. She bundled his T-shirt and shorts and shoved them into his gym bag. She looked at Rowan, who sat on the side of his bed looking miserable and a little bemused.

Battered and bruised and hopelessly sexy.

Jamie resisted the urge to kiss him again, to wrap her arms around him and tell him she was so glad he was okay, that nothing worse had happened to him. She loathed it when people she cared about were hurt.

Hated it when they died. *Don't go there, James.*

"Can you leave? Have you been discharged?"

"James…"

Jamie sighed at the stubborn look on his face, the flash of I've-got-this in his eyes. She sat down on the bed and threaded her fingers through his. "Look, I get that you don't like help, that you are used to doing stuff on your own. I understand that our lives are upside down right now and that neither of us knows how to deal with the pregnancy, our attraction or, frankly, with each other. We seem to be dancing out of step, to a different tune. I step forward, you step back and vice versa."

He nodded, his fingers squeezing hers.

"Can we agree to be more open with each other, Rowan?" she asked. "I want to come home with you because I can't bear the thought of you struggling when I can help you." She hauled in a deep breath and forced herself to speak the hard words. "I need to help you, Rowan."

Maybe that was because she couldn't help Kaden when he'd been hurt. Maybe she just wanted this independent, lonely man to have someone to rely on. Maybe she was being too emotional, setting herself up for a fall. Or maybe this was too real. But right now, she didn't care.

She wanted and needed to be with Rowan.

She lifted her eyebrows and waited for him to speak.

"Staying away has been hell. I want to make love to you again," he stated, his expression serious. "And I want to keep making love to you until this thing between us peters out."

Because, his eyes told her, it would gradually disappear. Of course it would; both of them were scared of commitment. She didn't want to love someone again and have it blow up in her face.

She forced herself to smile. "I like the sound of that song," she told him.

He tugged her forward to kiss her, his mouth promising magic. "Me too," Rowan told her, closing his eyes. "While I'd love you to take me home and ravish me, that's not going to happen today. I just feel so...shitty. And tired."

"I can't understand why," Jamie teased him. "You only had an operation a few hours ago, and the drugs are still working their way out of your system. You're probably going to sleep for the rest of the day."

Nurse Briggs appeared in the doorway, her hands resting on the handles of a wheelchair. She looked at Jamie, her eyes bright in her lined face. "Are you getting enough rest? Taking prenatal vitamins? Folic acid?"

Jamie's eyes widened, and she laid a hand on her stomach. How the hell did she *know*?

"Uh...um..." She cleared her throat. "How do you know that I'm pregnant?"

The nurse tapped her index finger against the side of her nose. "Been around for a long, long time. Well, are you?"

Knowing that she'd get a lecture, Jamie almost lied and told her she was taking vitamins. At the last minute, she shook her head and told her she wasn't. She nearly added that there was no point, but kept those words behind her teeth.

"You should," Nurse Briggs informed her. "You also need to rest and relax."

Jamie caught Rowan's eyes and saw the sympathy within them. She jerked her shoulders up to tell him that it didn't matter, that she was used to being disappointed. But a wave of longing smacked her in the heart. She wanted a baby. Specifically, she wanted Rowan's baby. She wanted to see his eyes in another's face, kiss the same square chin and long nose.

Damn, where had that come from?

"Are you okay?" Rowan asked her, standing up. He took a couple of steps toward her and gripped her biceps, concern on his face.

Jamie pulled herself together and looked up into his still-white face. "I should be asking you that."

He cupped her cheek and sent her a soft, slow smile. "We are quite a pair. Thank you for coming, by the way. Like everything else to do with you, it was…unexpected."

Unexpected. What a perfect word!

"Okay, wrap it up. I've got work to do. Put your fine ass in this chair, Mr. Cowper, and let me parade you through the hospital."

Rowan scowled at the chair before turning to look at Nurse Briggs and handing her his most charming smile. "I'm feeling much steadier on my feet, but I just need a few minutes with Jamie. So why don't you go grab a cup of coffee and come back for me in ten?"

She stared at him, eyes narrowed and lips pursed. "You're going to leg it, aren't you?"

Rowan's wide-eyed look was more fake than the flower arrangements in the hospital lobby. He placed a hand on his chest, looking wounded. "I'm hurt by your lack of trust."

"And I'm a freakin' leprechaun," Nurse Briggs muttered. She pulled the wheelchair out of the room and shook her head. "Coffee. I need coffee."

When they could no longer hear her footsteps, Rowan and Jamie legged it, hand in hand.

Eleven

When he woke up later, Rowan felt better, less like a rehydrated corpse and more like himself. Rolling onto his back, he checked his watch, saw that it was after seven in the evening—he'd slept for the better part of the day—and switched on his bedside lamp. Sitting up, he ran his uninjured hand through his messy hair, which was clean after Jamie had helped rinse it of blood. He'd washed up as best he could before tiredness and the aftereffects of the anesthesia forced him to find his bed.

Yawning, Rowan stood up and looked around his room. He'd always thought it cool and uncluttered, but he understood why Jamie thought it was a bit morgue-like. It was unrelentingly white.

Maybe he could hire an interior decorator to

bring in some color, maybe a plant or two. Right. That anesthesia must've hit him harder than he'd realized if he was thinking about redecorating just because Jamie didn't like his place.

Like everyone else, Jamie would leave his life eventually. Everyone he cared about always did. When she lost the baby, as she insisted she would, they'd move on. They'd both go back to the way they had been before—both skimming along the surface of love and life, both too damn scared to duck under the waves.

So changing anything—his apartment, his life, his attitude—was simply stupid. Nothing would come of them as a couple. Nothing could.

Unless she *didn't* miscarry his baby…

Rowan rubbed the back of his neck, realizing that he'd deliberately not thought about that possibility because she was so very convinced she couldn't carry a baby to term. But what if she did? What then? How would they move forward? What would she expect from him? What did he expect from himself?

Rowan sat down on the edge of the bed and stared at the hardwood floor. He'd be a father, a role model. How was he supposed to be either when he'd never had a dad or a role model himself?

He was cautious and cynical, deeply wary and unable to trust. How could he be expected to raise a well-balanced kid?

First things first: they needed to get past these next few weeks…

"Hey, you're awake."

He looked up to see Jamie standing in the doorway to his bedroom, still dressed in her work clothes—tailored gray pants and another of her silky T-shirts, this one a pale pink. Her makeup had worn off, and he could see freckles on her nose and the natural color of her lips. She looked messy, tired and utterly fantastic.

She stopped next to where he was sitting and looked down at his head, gently moving his hair to see his stitches. "How are you feeling?"

He inhaled her sexy scent and raised his hand to grip her hip, shuffling her so that she stood between his knees. He rested his forehead on her stomach and felt her hands stroking his shoulders, an action that was both soothing and arousing. "Thanks for staying, for looking after me. It's not something I'm used to, so if I was grumpy—" he shrugged, unable to look up at her "—sorry."

Jamie's fingers danced across the back of his neck, and he shivered. "Greg broke his arm when he was eight, and he whined like a spoiled little girl. You're behaving marginally better than him."

He abruptly lifted his head and pulled back to look at her. Had he been that bad? Jamie shook her head and smiled at him. "Relax, Cowper. I'm teasing you again. Have you never been teased before?"

He'd encountered it—of course he had—but it had always had a nasty edge, words that sliced deep. Jamie's teasing was light and sweet and held no malice. He had no way with words, but he knew he could tease in another way. He raised the hem of her shirt and placed his mouth against her warm tummy, painting her skin with soft kisses.

"What are you doing?" Jamie asked, her voice turning husky.

"Teasing you back. It's the only way I know how," he responded, surprised by his honesty. He dipped his tongue into her belly button. "How am I doing?"

"You could try a little harder," Jamie suggested, bending down to drop a kiss on his head.

Rowan felt that kiss down to his toes, warm and tender. He was used to sex, to affairs, to the tangle of limbs and chasing that orgasm high, but he'd never experienced gentle heat, tenderness and emotion when making love. He felt fear well up—fear of commitment, of being abandoned, of loving and losing another person—and pushed it away.

He wanted gentle, just once in his life. He wanted the slow and subtle and sweet.

He tipped his head back up to look into her lovely face, falling into the richness of her eyes. "Make love with me?"

"Are you…"

"I'm fine. I just…" He forced the words out. "I need you, Jamie. Be with me?"

She nodded, smiled and skimmed the back of her hand over his cheek. She stepped back and reached for the hem of her shirt, pulled it up and over her head. Her bra matched her shirt, shell pink—lacy and sexy and, God help him, low-cut. He watched, his heart in his throat, as she undid the button to her trousers, pushing the fabric down her round hips to reveal her slim, strong legs. Her high-cut panties matched her bra, the perfect foil for her olive-colored skin.

She was gorgeous, feminine and—for tonight—his.

Rowan stood and lifted his hands to cup her face, realized he could only use one hand and growled in frustration. Holding her face with that one hand, he lowered his head and covered her mouth with his, sighing as her lips softened under his. This woman, this moment… He couldn't get enough.

He deepened his kiss and ran his hand down her chest, cupped a breast and skimmed his thumb over her already-tight nipple. Doing this one-handed was a pain in the ass, but he'd manage. Curling his arm around her back, he yanked her up against him and kissed her deeper. He wanted her senseless, thinking only of him. Of how good they were together.

From a place far away, he felt Jamie open the buttons to his shirt, her hands exploring his back, his sides, burrowing under the band of his shorts to stroke his butt. Her touch electrified every inch of skin, and he fought the urge to rip off her panties and slide inside her.

He needed more than a quick bang tonight; he needed a connection. "Take off your bra, sweetheart, and get those panties off."

Jamie—panting softly, her skin flushed pink—

did as he'd asked, and then she was naked in his arms. The way he liked her best.

He bent down to suck a nipple into his mouth, mentally smiling when she gasped and arched her back to increase the intensity of his kiss. He felt her hips jerk and, in response to her silent plea, he slid his hand between her legs, seeking her hot, lovely, lush places. She was wet already, and when he touched her clit, she released a soft moan.

"I love the way you touch me, Row," she told him. "You haven't done nearly enough of it."

He pulled away to clock her dazed expression, taking in her closed eyes and the soft smile on her face. For as long as he lived, he'd remember the flush on her cheeks, the way her long eyelashes lay against her skin, the curl of her mouth.

He'd wanted to wait but couldn't—not anymore. Spinning her around, he pushed her down so that she sat on the edge of her bed, leaning back on her elbows. He pushed his shorts down his hips, cursed his button-down shirt and sighed when her hand closed around his shaft. He stood statue-still, loving the way her thumb brushed his tip, how she rolled him through her fingers.

"So strong. So masculine."

He felt strong, powerful—more of a man than he'd ever felt before. Loving this woman, being in her arms, made him feel…better than he'd ever felt before. He could stand here forever, watching her face as she touched him, wishing she'd take him in her mouth but knowing he wouldn't last ten seconds if she did.

She licked her lips and moved her head closer to him, and her tongue darted out to swirl around his head. Heaven. Hell.

He needed to be inside her. *Now.*

"Scoot up the bed," he told her, and when she did, he started to place his hands on the bed next to her and cursed out loud when he remembered his cast. *Shit!* How the hell was he going to support himself if he couldn't rest his weight on his hands? He was too heavy to put all his bulk on her.

Jamie pushed him away and quickly divested him of his shirt, releasing a low "mmm" of approval as she ran her arms over his bare chest and stomach.

"Roll on your back, Row," she told him, her bossy tone a turn-on. He was happy to oblige.

A second after his back hit the covers, she had one leg straddling his thighs, and then her core slid up and down his shaft. He barely managed to catch up when she took him in hand and slowly lowered herself onto him.

Being inside her was the best place to be. A lovely, wet, warm, safe place. But, God, they weren't using any condoms.

He stretched out his hand to pat the bedside table, looking for the handle of the drawer.

"What'cha doing, Cowper?" Jamie asked, rocking slightly and sending his blood pressure soaring.

It took some mental processing to find the word to answer her question. "Condom."

"Can't get pregnant twice," Jamie reminded him. "And I've been tested. I presume you have too?"

Caught up in the magic of being surrounded by her without a barrier, he could only think of one word: "Yeah."

"Then can we stop talking?" Jamie asked, bending down and giving him an open-mouth kiss.

"Yeah."

Rowan cupped the back of her head, pulled her down and slid his tongue into her mouth. He jerked his hips, pushing himself deeper. She whimpered and sighed and bore down on him, and he felt that familiar itching at the base of his spine—the wonderful buildup to what he was sure would be a mini cosmic bang.

Jamie sat up, her back straight, and he watched her ride him, glorious as she chased down her pleasure. Her hands came up to touch her breasts, and he found her clitoris, determined to make her fly, fast and hard.

He knew she was close—so was he—and when he felt her clench his cock, the burst of warmth and wetness against his tip, he allowed himself to let go, detonating into color and sensation.

Harder, deeper and by far the best he'd ever had.

He looked tired, Jamie decided as she slid a grilled cheese sandwich in front of him. She sat down next to him at the large white—of course— dining table on the other side of the marble island, her plate in her hand.

Then again, after a fall, an operation and fantastic sex—twice—it was no wonder the guy looked shattered. But Rowan had stamina; she had to give him that.

She picked up her sandwich, took a bite and cursed when a blob of cheese landed on the front of Rowan's shirt. After deciding they needed sustenance, they'd opted to forage for some food. Not comfortable with walking around, or cooking, naked, she pulled on a designer T-shirt she'd found in Rowan's dresser. There was now a grease stain on its pocket.

"Sorry," she said with a grimace, dabbing it with a paper napkin.

"I can't tell you how little I care," Rowan replied. He smiled at her, and her heart rolled over. "You look good in my shirt. Not as good as you look naked, but good."

She smiled. He was a guy who wasn't comfortable with giving compliments, so hearing one fall off his lips was an amazing gift. *He's different tonight,* Jamie thought, eyeing him as he demolished his sandwich. Softer, more emotionally available.

"Why didn't you call me, or anyone else, for help today, Row?" she asked, curious.

His eyes slammed into hers before looking down at his plate. His shoulders, now covered in a sky blue T-shirt, rose and fell. "As I said, it's because I'm very used to doing everything myself. There's never been anyone to call, Jamie," Rowan added, surprising her with that very personal piece of information.

What did he mean? "Nobody? A friend? A cousin? An ex-girlfriend?"

"No, no one. I have friends. I'm not a recluse, but there's nobody I feel comfortable asking for help." He held up his hand, and she saw the defiance in his eyes. "I don't need your pity!"

"I'm just trying to understand, Row," Jamie told him, keeping her voice steady and calm. "Most people have *someone*."

"I don't." He sighed, bundled his napkin into a ball and pushed his plate away. He rested his forearms on the table and leaned forward. "My mom took off when I was twelve, and she wasn't what I'd call responsible. She was always high, and I was in and out of foster care as a young kid. Then I went in permanently the year I turned twelve. I moved maybe eight times over the next six years."

Dear God. She'd moved once, had transferred from one school to another, and that had been hard enough. Eight times? That was inconceivable.

"Look, you don't need to be a psychologist to realize that being unsettled makes it difficult to bond with people," Rowan explained. "My mother's antics were nothing compared to how difficult it was to move."

"Were they nice places? Was that why it was difficult to leave them?" Jamie asked, trying to understand.

"No. Some of them were pretty awful," he admitted. "I mean, I wasn't beaten or abused—"

Something flashed in his eyes, and Jamie suspected that while he was speaking the truth, he might've come close to experiencing both horrors. She placed her hands on her stomach, tasting fear in the back of her throat for the child he'd been.

"Moving was difficult because I felt constantly unsettled. I could never plan. I was always worried about what came next. I'd learn the rules, figure out how to exist in a space; and then I'd be moved, and I'd have to figure a new set of rules, a new space." He picked up his glass, sipped and put it down again. "There was one family I kind of bonded with, just a little. They were awesome, and I was just starting to drop some walls. I think it was my second move, so I must've been thirteen or so. Then, out of the blue, my foster dad was transferred to another state. They couldn't take me out of state, and losing them nearly killed me. After that, I kept my distance. I still do, so that's why I find it difficult to ask for help."

Jamie nodded, understanding that on a deeper level, he was terrified of relationships, of any type, because he didn't want to be abandoned again. So it was easier not to create bonds, to pull away before anyone got hurt—especially him.

Didn't she do the same but for different reasons? She didn't allow herself to form attachments to men because she was terrified of loss. She'd lost four babies and a husband. The miscarriages were a quirk of nature, but *she* was responsible for Kaden's death.

She couldn't blame Rowan for distancing himself. She really couldn't. Why wouldn't one, as a sensible and intelligent person, try and avoid that which had scoured one before?

It just made sense, didn't it?

They were quite the pair.

Both scared, both damaged, both fighting the pull of their deep, profound attraction.

Well, she definitely was. And Jamie suspected Rowan was too.

Twelve

Another two weeks passed, and they were still sleeping together. And, yes, their friends, family and the general population of Annapolis believed they were a couple.

Neither she nor Rowan could be bothered to explain what they were or weren't. Mostly because neither of them knew. Or, at least, Jamie didn't.

After kissing Rowan's shoulder, Jamie slid out of her bed, pulled on a short robe and pattered down the hall to her kitchen. Yawning, she sleepily checked the level of the water and beans in her coffee machine and hit the button to power it up. Rowan would want coffee when he woke up, but she'd settle for tea. She and Rowan hadn't had much sleep last night—why sleep when they could make love?—and she was exhausted.

But that could also be the pregnancy hormones kicking in. She hadn't experienced any morning sickness yet, but she remembered the bone-deep tiredness she'd felt with her other pregnancies, always worse in the week before she miscarried. It would happen soon, of that she was sure.

And then either she or Rowan would start finding excuses to put some distance between them. Work would suddenly become a priority, and seeing each other every night of the week would dwindle to three times a week, then two, then nothing.

They might exchange a few text messages, a couple of emails; and in six months, a year, they'd bump into each other at a function and have an awkward conversation, exchange some strained small talk. He might be with a date; she probably wouldn't be.

It was all quite sad, really, because she and Rowan enjoyed each other, out of bed as well as in. They both loved word games, preferred books to TV, and rock to country. Their politics were mostly the same, and neither felt the need to fill extended silences with inanities. They were comfortable together, Jamie realized. Yet one look, one touch, could fire up the sizzle, and they'd start ripping off clothes.

But it would end—it would have to. Soon. Nothing lasted forever, and neither would this. Love, like, attraction—it was all as fragile as spun sugar. It shattered, dissolved, disappeared.

Jamie heard her phone chime, and she picked it up to read the text message.

So looking forward to seeing you all tomorrow afternoon. It's been too long!

She grimaced, remembering that she'd accepted the invitation to a baby shower months ago. Alice, the mother-to-be, was the wife of Kaden's brother, and a couple they'd spent a lot of time with back in the day. They'd had a huge group of friends, most of whom she'd lost touch with.

She must've been feeling sentimental when the invitation had dropped into her inbox, or nostalgic, or lonely.

"Hey."

Jamie looked up to see Rowan walking into the room, dressed in a pair of boxer shorts and a plain white T-shirt. He made a beeline for the coffee maker before stopping to plant a kiss on her temple. "You okay?" he asked after yawning. He gestured to her phone. "Bad news?"

She leaned back against the counter as he pulled two mugs out of the cupboard above the coffee maker. "Irritating news."

Rowan shoved a cup under the spout and hit the button with the side of his fist. "Why, what's up? Do you want tea?"

"Yes, please. Months ago, I agreed to go to a baby shower tomorrow afternoon. The expectant mother is Kaden's sister-in-law."

"And the problem is...?"

Where to start? She sat down at her dining table and lifted her heels onto the seat of her chair. "We have nothing in common anymore. We are nothing more than Facebook friends, and I don't know if I can spend an afternoon talking about babies."

"You have your husband in common," Rowan pointed out as he placed her cup of tea next to her elbow. "They must miss him. And you."

She shrugged. Of course they missed Kaden. She still missed him! But none of them would want her around if they knew what she'd done.

Rowan sat down opposite her, his coffee cup dwarfed by his big hand. "What happened, James?"

"What do you mean?"

Rowan's eyes didn't leave her face. "I know from experience that people talk far more about the good things in the past, and we rarely talk about the bad stuff. We never talk about the *really* bad stuff. I think I've heard you mention your husband just a handful of times since I met you."

"I don't feel comfortable talking about my dead husband to my part-time lover," Jamie retorted, feeling panicky.

"Was your marriage so awful?" Rowan persisted.

"No! I mostly had a great marriage. He was a lovely guy," she replied, feeling stung that he would think that.

"Then why don't you talk about him? If not to me, then to Greg and your family?"

Her hand tightened around her mug. "Have you been discussing me with my brother?"

"Discussing? No. But he talks and I listen." Rowan sipped, but his eyes remained laser-sharp on her face. "So why don't you talk about him, James?"

"Goddammit, Rowan, let it go!" Jamie shouted at him.

He remained calm and unfazed. "I would if I thought *you* could. Tell me what happened, Jamie. Because it's eating you up inside."

How did he know that? How was it that he knew her so well after such a short time? And why was she so tempted to tell him the truth? Because she was sick of keeping the secret to herself or was it because she trusted that Rowan, who didn't have a rosy worldview, wouldn't judge her too harshly?

The words were bubbling up, and Jamie placed her hand on her throat, to push them back down again. Once they were out, she'd have to deal with the fallout—Rowan's reaction and her emotions.

"Tell me, sweetheart."

Jamie stared at the wooden surface of the table and ran her finger up and down the handle of her cup. Could she cross this line? Maybe, but only with him.

"After years of fertility issues, losing the babies, we were struggling. Kaden wanted his own kid, his own flesh and blood. He didn't want to adopt or use a surrogate. He wanted a baby the old-fashioned way. I couldn't go through another miscarriage, and we were at an impasse. It got to a point where that was all he wanted to talk about, and whenever he raised the subject, I walked out of the room. We were so unhappy."

Rowan just watched her, his expression calm and implacable. He lifted his coffee cup in a "carry on" gesture. So she did.

"He arranged a weekend away, something to re-ignite the spark. He told me that we weren't going to discuss anything serious. We were just going to have fun, make love, eat, make more love. Concentrate on each other and not the problems." Jamie swallowed, her skin suddenly too small for her body. "I was ridiculously excited and so appreciative. We were going to reset our marriage. He'd made reservations at an inn, and it was snowing. Our trip started well, and I was excited. But within a half hour, he raised the subject of me trying, one more time, to get pregnant.

"I was furious and I felt like he'd ambushed me. We had a four-hour drive, and I couldn't get out of the car and leave. I told him I didn't want to talk about it, that I'd had four miscarriages and I didn't want to go through another. But he wouldn't stop talking, trying to get me to change my mind." She shrugged. "I lost it. I started screaming at him, telling him he was a selfish bastard, that he was bullying me, and to turn the car around. He started yelling back, and the next thing I remember was being stuck in a crumpled car and watching the light fade from his eyes."

"James." The word was coated with empathy,

and when she raised her head to look at Rowan, his normally tough face was soft. "I'm so sorry."

"It's my fault he died. I shouldn't have lost my temper. I shouldn't have yelled or told him that I wanted a divorce. I was just so angry."

"He should've kept his word about not discussing the subject and given you the weekend he promised you," Rowan softly countered.

"And you both should've known better than to discuss such an emotional subject while driving in icy conditions," Rowan stated, his voice so calm and nonjudgmental that Jamie couldn't take offense. "You were both wrong, in different ways. As for him dying? That was an accident, James. Not your fault, not his. Just a horrible quirk of fate."

She wanted to believe him—she did. And, intellectually, she could see his reasoning. But it would take a while for her heart to catch up to her brain. If it ever did.

Jamie pulled her bottom lip between her teeth. "Maybe if I'd just agreed to try again, he'd be alive."

Rowan, surprising her, nodded. "Yeah, maybe he would be alive. But if you'd done that and lost another baby, you would've hated him and felt doubly resentful and angry. You can't play the 'what if' game, Jamie."

Couldn't she? She was rather good at it.

Rowan pushed his coffee cup away and tapped his finger on his cast. "Having had this discussion, I need to tell you how sorry I am about you being pregnant, Jamie. I could kick myself because

I would never put you through pain or distress if I could help it."

Jamie placed her hand on his and squeezed. "I know that, Row. I do. Yeah, the miscarriage is going to suck, but I knew that from the moment I did that test. But we're not married, neither of us wants to be in a permanent relationship and there's no pressure on us." She made herself smile, then lie. "You're not in love with me, and I'm not in love with you."

Jamie waited for the lightning bolt to strike her, and when it didn't, she figured she had the universe's permission to carry on fudging the truth.

"We like each other, but we both know that at some point we'll drift apart, as we were always supposed to do."

God, the idea was a stake through her heart. How was she going to wake up alone instead of being curled up against his hot, muscled body? Who would she talk to about anything and nothing? How was she going to fill the empty spaces in her home and life after he left?

But she had to let him go…

He'd always been destined to leave. She might've changed her mind on taking a chance—or was considering it—but she knew he hadn't.

Rowan's expression was enigmatic, and after a couple of seconds—or maybe a hundred, who knew?—he stood up slowly and walked around to where she sat. He bent down and placed a lingering kiss on her temple, then her mouth.

"Thank you for telling me," he said, his voice a

whisper against her lips. "And I am so, so sorry I put you in this position."

What position? Losing her baby?

Or breaking her heart?

Rowan stood in Jamie's shower, the bathroom door closed and locked. He rested his forearm on the tiles above his head, conscious of a deep, pervasive sadness he'd never experienced before. Up until this conversation, the subject of a miscarriage had been an intellectual exercise. It hadn't touched him emotionally. But in the last fifteen minutes, he'd connected with the idea that his kid was inside her, fighting for a place in this world. And that he, or she, probably wouldn't make it.

He knew he'd never grasp the full impact of a miscarriage. He wasn't a pregnant person, and he'd never properly get it. He'd never know the soul-deep sadness, the connection she'd had with her other babies and with the one inside her. He'd never pretend to...

But losing the baby wasn't all that was on his mind.

His guilt about impregnating Jamie was fighting a war with his realization that theirs wasn't just an I-think-you're-hot attraction anymore. Yes, he couldn't keep his hands off her. They made love often, and it was mind-blowing, but he loved their quiet moments too. Holding her as she slept was a pleasure he'd never experienced before. Hearing her laugh lifted his soul. He liked the person he was with her—calmer, less stressed, quick to laugh, strangely affectionate.

"You're not in love with me, and I'm not in love with you."

As she'd said those words, every cell in his body vibrated, yelling for him to refute her statement. The truth hit him—hard and fast—that he *was* in love with her and that she was the only person he could imagine building a life with, committing to—loving.

He loved her.

Hard to admit because he was so damn scared of losing her, but he couldn't lie to himself any longer. He'd kept coming back to her because his soul recognized hers. She was the big hole in his life he'd always had trouble filling.

He didn't want to go create a family with anyone other than Jamie. Maybe they wouldn't have kids that were genetically theirs, but he honestly didn't care if they adopted or used a surrogate. He just wanted a family with Jamie at the center of it.

But she'd made it very clear that she was better off on her own, that she neither wanted nor desired more kids or a committed relationship. He got it. She'd been married, had experienced a great loss. But he couldn't trust anyone else with his heart, his life, his kids.

It was either Jamie or no one.

And since she'd just told him she didn't love him and that she didn't want a permanent relationship, he was facing the lonely, empty life he'd thought he wanted.

Rowan rested the back of his head against the shower tiles. What should he do? How should he go forward? If he pushed her for more, told her he loved her, asked her to consider a life with him, wouldn't he be just like her ex, who'd pushed his agenda when she told him, time and again, that wasn't what she wanted?

Or should he just give her time and space, let her drive the pace of their relationship, and hope her barriers would break down and she'd let him in?

He was a guy who liked action, who worked for what he wanted, but he couldn't *make* her love him. She either did or she didn't, would or wouldn't. So, for now, he'd just stand here and curse in the shower, where no one could hear him.

They were living on eggshells, and it was making them both irritable and sensitive, Rowan thought as he walked into Jamie's kitchen early one morning. He rubbed his hand through his hair and headed to the coffee maker, intent on getting some caffeine into his system. He'd persuaded the orthopedic surgeon to remove his cast a little early, and was enjoying a wider range of movement, especially in bed.

He and Jamie might not be talking much—a wall the size of Texas had sprung up between them since she'd told him about her husband's death—but that hadn't stopped them from turning to each other in the night.

Last night had been a marathon session, and he was exhausted. A good exhausted, admittedly.

He'd toyed with the idea of yanking down that wall and telling her, openly and honestly, that no matter what happened with the baby, he wanted to stick around. That he loved her. But, judging by her remote expression, she wasn't ready to go there. He swallowed down his impatience and reminded himself that love couldn't be bulldozed through.

But Rowan also knew they couldn't keep on like this. Something had to break. And soon.

"I'll have another cup, thanks."

Rowan jumped at the deep voice and spun around. But instead of an intruder, Greg sat at Jamie's dining table, looking uncharacteristically sweaty.

Had he been running?

Rowan put his hands on his thighs and heaved in some air, trying to get his heart rate to slow. "For the love of God! What the hell?"

Greg grinned at him. "Morning. Are you always this unobservant, or did I catch you on a bad day?"

Rowan straightened and glared at him. "I wasn't expecting you at oh-dark-hundred, sitting in Jamie's kitchen."

"I am her brother," Greg mildly pointed out before nodding to the coffee maker. "Are you going to make me one, or do I have to make my own?"

"I'm on it," Rowan grumbled, turning back to the coffee. As he completed the familiar actions, his heart rate dropped and his breathing evened out. He carried the cups over to the table and handed Greg his before taking the seat opposite him.

"Is letting yourself into her house something you regularly do, or is this a special occasion?"

"Before you arrived on the scene, I used to make it over here a couple of times a week," Greg told him. "Lately, I thought I'd give you guys some privacy."

"Nice of you," Rowan replied dryly. "And it's a good thing I don't walk around the house naked." Rowan lifted his cup to his lips, took a reviving sip and sighed. How did people start the day with tea? Or nothing? It made no damn sense.

He looked at Greg, so at home in Jamie's house. "So what's different today?"

Greg's finger traced the lip of his cup and his sherry-colored eyes, so like Jamie's, turned to chestnut brown. He frowned before asking his straight-as-an-arrow question. "What's going on with you and Jamie?"

Rowan held his cup to his lips, surprised by the question. "What do you mean?"

"You came to dinner the night before last and you were both acting...weird."

Weird? He and Jamie had laughed, joked and talked, both determined to show Greg and Chas that everything was fine. They'd acted their asses off, but it seemed neither of them would be receiving an award for their performance.

"We were acting perfectly normally," Rowan protested, mostly because he thought he should.

"While we were in the room, you two laughed and joked, but when we left, you had nothing to say to each other."

Damn. "How do you know that?"

"We spied on you," Greg retorted. "Stood at the door and peeked through, ears flapping. They say that eavesdroppers don't hear anything good about themselves, but we didn't hear anything at all. In fact, it reminds me of how Jamie and Kaden were in the months before his death." Greg nailed Rowan with a hard look. "Has she told you about Kaden?"

"Yes," Rowan replied. When Greg's eyes brightened, he shook his head. "And, no, I'm not telling you."

Greg pulled a face. "I'm presuming you won't tell me what's going on with you two either?"

"Nope."

"Is she going to get hurt?" Greg asked, and Rowan appreciated his blunt question.

Losing the baby was going to hurt like hell, but losing him? Not so much. "Yeah, probably. If it's any consolation, I will not escape unscathed either."

Greg pushed his hands into his hair and rubbed his scalp. "You two make life so damn complicated! You're crazy about her, she's crazy about you—"

He didn't need a lecture, especially at this hour of the day. "Greg, shut the hell up, okay?" Greg's head shot up, and he narrowed his eyes at Rowan. Rowan didn't give a crap. Ignoring the other man's annoyance, he leaned forward. "I need you to do me a favor—"

He didn't allow Greg the opportunity to refuse. "I'm leaving for Nashville today. I'll be there for the next few days. Matt and I are hammering out our vision for development, mostly so we can give our pain-in-the-ass architect something to work from."

"Shouldn't I be there? Wouldn't that save time?" Greg demanded.

It would, but he had other plans for Jamie's brother. Plans far more important than some architect drawings. "It would but I need you and Chas here. I need you to keep an eye on Jamie for me."

"Why?" Greg asked, instantly suspicious. "What's wrong with her?"

He couldn't explain, not without breaking Jamie's confidence. But the hell of it was, he didn't trust Jamie to let him know she was miscarrying.

Like him, she didn't like to ask for help. He suspected that when it happened, she'd go to the doctor or hospital by herself, deal with it on her own. If he couldn't be around, then he needed somebody close to her, someone he trusted, to hold her hand.

He refused for this to be just another thing she "handled."

"Look, I can't tell you, not without breaking a confidence, and I don't want to do that. I can tell you that she isn't in any danger—Jesus, will you be around or not?"

Greg stared at him, a slow smile creeping up his face and hitting his eyes. "You are so in love with her."

Yeah, yeah… So? And he was not having this

conversation with Jamie's brother. He glanced at the oversize clock on Jamie's scarlet-colored kitchen wall.

"Is that the time? I need to get going." He pushed his chair back, put his hands on his hips and gave Greg a hard stare. "So will you?"

He nodded and Rowan closed his eyes, relieved.

"What is Greg going to do?" Jamie asked, walking into her kitchen with messy hair and wearing one of Rowan's T-shirts. She stopped and stared at her brother. "Hopefully he's going to stop breaking into my house."

Greg replied that he had a key, and when the siblings started to bicker, Rowan took that as his cue to leave. The sooner he got to Nashville and completed his business, the sooner he could get back home.

Because home was wherever Jamie was.

Thirteen

In Nashville, Rowan sat on the edge of his bed, looking into his phone, and Jamie sighed. He looked so incredibly good in his mint-colored collared shirt, a black-and-white geometric tie lying against his chest. She, by contrast, looked like a train wreck.

Over the past few days, she'd started to lose color in her face and felt desperately tired. She knew the time was near.

"I wish I was with you. I'm sorry this trip is taking longer than I thought. I'd fly back now, but I have meetings this morning and this afternoon," Rowan told her, looking frustrated.

Over the past few weeks, Rowan had started coming home—to her place, not his—earlier and earlier, and some afternoons he even beat her home. He'd cooked for her, ran her bubble baths, rubbed her feet and had, on more than one occasion, carried her up to bed when she fell asleep on the couch watching TV. He was taking care of her and, God, how she liked it. No—she loved it.

When he walked out of her life—because he was going to at some point down the line—how was she going to handle it?

Badly. Very badly indeed.

She'd tried so hard to put up barriers between them, to create boundaries, but Rowan, who'd never met an obstacle he couldn't overcome, just barged through them. She kept retreating, emotionally and mentally—trying to find a way to safeguard her heart, to stop herself from falling in love with him—but nothing seemed to work.

And, man, she couldn't resist his touch. One kiss, one stroke of his hand, and she was lost...

She had to call it, and soon. She was at the top of a slippery hill, hanging on to a thin tree branch, teetering, about to slide down and collide with love. If she allowed herself to let go, her world would spin out of control. And when she came to a stop at the bottom of that exhilarating ride—when he left her—she'd feel like she'd broken every part of her body.

She knew what devastation felt like, and if she couldn't stop herself from falling in love with him now, she was on track to walk through that hellscape again.

Not if she could help it.

"Why don't you take the day off, sweetheart?" Rowan asked her. Why did he have to be so sweet, so considerate? Why couldn't he just be a normal, selfish, unobservant man? How was she supposed to resist him?

"Like your business needs you, mine needs me."

"I'm just suggesting that you get some rest," Rowan replied in a far-too-reasonable tone.

"Stop fussing, Rowan!" she snapped, knowing she was being irrational. She could blame her hormones—they were all over the place—but he was being everything a life partner should be: involved, engaged, kind.

It was far too real and too much.

Jamie felt her stomach cramp, and it was followed by a warm feeling between her legs. She knew that feeling. She placed the face of her phone against her forehead and wished it was all different.

Wished that this baby had stuck, that they both weren't so damn screwed up and terrified of love...

"James? What's going on?"

She lowered the phone, and her heart lurched at the panic in his eyes. If she didn't know better, she'd think that he loved her.

But she did know better.

He didn't love her. Couldn't. Never would.

"I've started to miscarry, Row. I felt... Well, I think it's starting."

"Jesus!" he shouted, leaping to his feet, panic flying across his face. "Okay, if you call an ambulance, I'll call Chas, tell him to get his ass over to your place—"

"Rowan—"

He shoved his hand into his hair. "I'll book the next flight out. I'll be there as soon as possible."

Jamie tipped her head to the side, feeling flat and dull. "Why?"

"What do you mean 'why'?" Rowan demanded.

"I've done this before, Rowan. I go to the ob-gyn, she examines me and I have a scan," Jamie explained. "I have a quick procedure and come home. There's nothing for you to do."

You could love me. I could love you. But neither of us is brave enough to let that happen.

"I can damn well be there for you, James!" Rowan bellowed.

Jamie briefly closed her eyes. "What's the point of you flying back here and holding my hand? It's not going to stop the miscarriage. And when it's all over, you'll fuss for a couple of days, and then, when things get back to normal, you'll look around and wonder what you are doing in my life and I'll wonder what I'm doing in yours. We'll make love, and it won't be the same as it was before. And one of us—maybe you, maybe me—will call it, and we'll go our separate ways."

Rowan scowled. "Why are we discussing our future breakup in the middle of you miscarrying?" he demanded. He released a sigh and scrubbed his face with his free hand. "But you're right. We can't carry on like this, James. We do need to talk."

Wasn't that code for "it's time to call it quits"? And, yep, it did hurt. More than she expected it to. She nodded. "We'll talk. But don't hurry back, Rowan. I've got this."

Rowan gave her a long, hard stare and shook his head before disconnecting. She didn't know if he was coming or staying in Nashville, whether to expect him or not.

Right, well… Okay, then. While she waited to find out, she had things to do. An ob-gyn to see. A broken heart to nurse.

Jamie sat in her darkened living room, her hands between her knees, staring at the black-and-white image on the coffee table in front of her, her heart thumping ten times its normal speed. Thinking she might pass out, she looked away and felt her pulse drop. Then she looked at the image again, and her heart rate accelerated once more.

At this rate, she'd need a pacemaker…

And sometime in the future…*maternity clothes*.

She was pregnant—miraculously still pregnant—and the small, grainy black-and-white print-out was the proof of her new reality.

She'd seen her baby's heartbeat, watched as the doctor took measurements, listened as she'd been given an estimated due date.

She and her baby were fine. They'd made it longer than any other pregnancy, and the doctor felt that the danger had passed and that there was no reason to worry. She was going to be a mama.

At the thought, Jamie burst into tears. Again.

Greg walked into the room, holding a tea tray, followed by Chas who rushed over to her. He sat on the arm of her chair and rubbed her back. "Take a deep breath, honey," he told her, pushing tissues into her hand.

Jamie looked up at him. "You saw the heartbeat, right?"

Chas nodded as he squeezed into the space next to her. "I did. You have a happy, healthy baby, Jamie darling."

Jamie released a sigh of relief, leaned into him and closed her eyes. What a day!

After her call to Rowan, she'd dressed and brushed her teeth, then called her ob-gyn. She was told to come in immediately and that they'd decide the next steps after she'd been examined. When she got to the doctor's, she'd found Greg and Chas waiting for her, having been sent by Rowan. She tried a few excuses to get Greg and Chas to leave, but they had just stared at her, eyebrows raised and feet planted. Eventually, she just blurted out the truth. "I'm pregnant and I'm about to miscarry."

"How do you know that?" Greg had demanded.

"I've miscarried before, remember?"

Greg had closed his eyes, looking devastated. "Shit, James. You should've told us you were pregnant."

She should've told them lots of things.

After she'd been examined, her ob-gyn took her for an ultrasound. Greg and Chas followed her and the doctor into a windowless room and crowded around the tiny screen, fascinated, as the doctor made some measurements and then traced the outline of her baby. When she'd pointed to the tiny, fluttering heartbeat, they all cried.

It was now midafternoon; her brothers were still hovering, and she still had to speak to Rowan, who'd texted that he would be with her by four o'clock. She took the cup of tea Greg held out, wrinkling her nose at his serious expression.

"You are going to tell him about the baby, right?"

"Of course I am," Jamie responded. She just didn't know how to explain the 360-degree change in circumstances. She'd told Rowan, over and over again, that there wouldn't be a baby, that he wasn't going to be a father; so she had no idea how he was going to take the news.

Sure, there was a possibility that she might still miscarry—there always was in any pregnancy—but her ob-gyn had said it was very unlikely. Her baby was strong and healthy. And, weirdly, Jamie knew her child was fine. She *felt* it.

"Be honest with him, James," Greg told her.

What did that mean? Of course she'd be honest with him. But she certainly wasn't stupid enough to believe that anything would change. She wouldn't be living in a roses-and-champagne world after she told him he was going to be a father. Rowan didn't want a relationship, and he certainly didn't want a relationship and a kid.

That morning, she'd been scared of falling in

love with Rowan and having him leave her, but now she had an additional reason to call their relationship quits. Whether she loved him or not—and she probably did but couldn't make herself admit it because it was too damn painful—she didn't want him to be with her for the sake of their child. She needed him to want to be with *her*, with or without a child. But since she'd fallen for the most independent, emotionally distant man she'd ever met, that wouldn't happen.

No, it was kinder to him—and to her—to let him go. If he wanted to, he could be part of their child's life. If Rowan decided fatherhood wasn't for him, her kid would have Greg and Chas, and her dad, as great male role models.

The growly sound of an expensive engine broke their silence, and Jamie placed a hand on her stomach, panic rising. Greg and Chas rose to their feet, exchanging a long look. Greg bent down and kissed Jamie's cheek. "While part of me wants to stay, I know this is something you need to do on your own. We'll go out the back door."

Jamie heard the slam of a car door and then the faint slide of his key in the front door. The sound of his bags dropping to the wooden floor echoed through the house, and Jamie sucked in a deep breath, then another.

"James? Where are you?" Rowan called as he tossed his keys into the pottery bowl by the door.

When she whispered his name, he turned and strode into the living room, still dressed in his dark gray suit and mint-colored shirt. He looked big and powerful and lovely.

His mouth curved up, and those amazing blue eyes lightened. "There you are. Hi."

Jamie touched her top lip with her tongue before responding. "Hi."

He bent down to brush his mouth across hers, then sat on the heavy wooden box that served as her coffee table and placed his big hands on her knees. "You're looking pale. Everything okay?"

Yep, that was her opening...

"So, as you know, I saw the ob-gyn this morning because I thought I was miscarrying."

Pain flashed in his eyes. "I'm sorry I wasn't here, James. Are you okay? How are you feeling? Shouldn't you still be in the hospit—wait, did you say you *thought* you were miscarrying?"

She nodded slowly.

"So you didn't miscarry?" Rowan asked, frowning.

She shook her head.

Impatience flickered across his face, settled in his eyes. "James, stop being cryptic. What is going on?"

She stood up and looked around, wanting to delay this moment. "Do you want a drink? A beer? Whiskey?"

"I'm fine," Rowan growled.

"I think you need a whiskey," Jamie insisted. "Trust me on this."

"I *need* you to sit your ass down and tell me what's going on!"

It was easier to show than tell, so Jamie pulled the ultrasound image from underneath his powerful thigh and handed it to him. She watched as he looked at it, turned it around and looked at it again. He even checked the back before shrugging. "I know this is a picture from an ultrasound machine, but I have no idea what I am looking at," he admitted.

Right. Time for explanations. "That's my baby, Rowan. The child you made with me. That kidney-shaped blob is my thirteen-week-old baby. That's his—or her—head, the spine. I saw and heard the heartbeat."

He looked from her to the picture and back to her face, his expression completely confused. "Are you telling me that the baby is viable?"

Jamie placed her hand on her stomach. "Not just viable—my baby is thriving."

Rowan rested the picture on his knee and pushed both his hands into his hair, staring down at it. "But you said you thought you were miscarrying."

Jamie raised her shoulders. "I had some blood, and I assumed it was just beginning. I went to the doctor immediately. I haven't had any spotting since, so she said it's nothing to worry about."

She could see his mind spinning. "Did the doctor explain why you haven't miscarried this time around like you did last time?"

"The most rational explanation is that there was a chromosomal issue between Kaden and me. She wanted to run those tests years ago, but Kaden always refused."

Rowan nodded. "Holy shit, Jamie."

Yeah, that was one way to put it.

He looked up, and the muscles around his eyes tightened, deepening the crow's-feet at the edges, and a huge smile, one she'd never seen before, transformed his face, making him look years younger. "Oh my God, we're going to have a baby!"

She wanted to roll around in his happiness, fling herself into his arms, fly away on his excitement. But she knew that when the initial shock died down and he realized the true implications of her being pregnant, he wouldn't be nearly as thrilled.

She'd just upended his calm, stable life. He'd never wanted a relationship, a commitment or kids; he was just responding to the moment. He wasn't being sensible.

She couldn't bear to taste happiness, to be filled by it and then have it ripped away.

He pulled her into his arms, whirled her around and dropped a hard kiss on her mouth. When she didn't respond, either with a kiss or to wrap her arms around his neck, he tensed and slowly lowered her to the floor. When she looked at him, his eyes radiated confusion.

"What is it? Why aren't you excited? You're having a baby!"

She touched her stomach, nodding. "I am." She sucked in a breath and lifted her shoulders to her ears. "But that doesn't necessarily mean that you are going to be a father."

His thick eyebrows pulled down. "What the hell do you mean by that?"

Jamie put some distance between them and folded her arms. "Look, I know this is a shock, but you need time to process this, to decide what you want."

Rowan pushed his jacket back to place his hands on his hips. "What the hell do you mean by *that*?" he demanded again.

"You're excited now, but in a few days, a few months, you might not be. I'm perfectly happy raising this kid myself, Rowan."

"Good God, I cannot believe I am hearing this! Why are you acting like this?"

Because she didn't want him to promise her the world and then decide he couldn't give her an inch of it. Because she'd been let down before, and she'd rather have her heart dinged now than shattered later. She raised her chin, looking defiant. "What? Are you going to offer to marry me?" she asked, her tone scathing.

"Yeah, I would marry you."

Thought so. "But only because of the baby! We agreed this wasn't a long-term thing, that it wasn't going to get serious!"

If he wouldn't go, then she would have to push him away. It was the only way to protect herself. She loved him, but she knew the consequences of love, knew how devastating it could be when it was lost forever. She'd loved Kaden, but what she had felt for him paled beside what she could feel for Rowan—if she dropped all her protective barriers.

He was everything she wanted in a man, a partner and a lover. Hardworking, smart, loving, occasionally frustrating. Sexy as hell. Her love for him was a massive wave behind a cracked seawall, desperately trying to find a path through. She had to keep it back or else it would drown her.

The anger died in Rowan's eyes, replaced by an icy intensity she'd never seen before. "Are you trying to tell me that you're not interested in making a relationship work?"

She spread her fingers apart. "I don't want us getting sucked into this false bliss and then realizing we're wrong for each other! It's better to accept that now and go back to being who we were before—two people living their lives solo."

She saw the flicker of fire in his eyes, followed by despair, and fought the urge to apologize. A little hurt now would save a lot of pain down the line. For him and for her.

He wasn't the settling-down type, she reminded herself. He'd never once suggested he wanted more. Until now. She was protecting herself. She was allowed to do that, wasn't she?

"You're dumping me?" Rowan asked in an ultrapolite voice.

Damn, when he put it like that… "I just don't want us to have unrealistic expectations of the future. You're not a settling-down type guy, and I don't want another relationship! But you're welcome to have a relationship with this baby, if you want."

"Good of you," Rowan told her, his voice scalpel-sharp. "Just to be clear—you might not want me, James, but I want that kid!"

"It's not that I—" Jamie spluttered, then pushed her palms into her eye sockets. She was over-whelmed with emotion: happiness, terror, sadness. And all she wanted, confusingly, was Rowan to take her in his arms and tell her it would be okay, that they would be okay. That they'd make it work, no matter what life flung at them.

Instead of scooping her up, Rowan sent her an-other icy look and walked the short distance into the hall. He picked up his keys and his overnight bag and pushed his phone into the inside pocket of his jacket. She didn't want him to go, but she was too scared to ask him to stay.

Rowan reached for the doorknob and opened her front door, turning back to look at her. "I've spent my life expecting people to disappoint me, James. But, stupidly, I never expected you to."

His words were a series of poison-tipped arrows to her heart. Jamie felt her knees buckle, and her vision began to swim. From a place far away, she saw her front door close behind him. She dropped to her knees and bent forward, hot tears dripping onto her hardwood floor.

Both Greg and Chas were sitting at her breakfast table when she came down the next morning, and the first thing she noticed was a bottle of champagne sitting in a silver ice bucket on her table. Champagne flutes, a jug of orange juice and a basket of fluffy croissants completed the early-morning picnic.

Jamie wanted to vomit, and not because she was pregnant. "You guys need to learn to phone ahead," she told them, heading for the kettle.

Chas walked over to her, pulled her in for a hug and kissed her head. "How's our favorite mama this morning?"

She had no idea how to answer that question. Luckily, Greg jumped in with a question of his own. "Where's Rowan? How did he take the news? Is he still asleep? In the shower? Is he thrilled?"

Jamie, not knowing how to answer, burst into tears. She held on to Chas's shirt and sobbed, her shoulders heaving. Chas, bless him, simply held on.

When she finally lifted her head off his chest, the champagne bottle and the glasses were gone and Greg had made her a cup of tea. She didn't want tea. She wanted Rowan.

Chas led her over to a chair, sat her down and pushed the cup toward her. "Drink. You've lost about six liters crying."

She wanted to smile at his exaggeration but couldn't. She took the paper towel Greg had thrust at her and wiped her eyes, then blew her nose. "I think Rowan and I are done."

"Why do you think that?" Chas asked gently.

"And what did you do?" Greg demanded with a deep scowl.

"Why do you automatically assume it's me?" Jamie asked him, feeling stung.

Greg snorted his disbelief. "Because that man is besotted. He would move heaven and earth for you!"

"Greg," Chas chided. He reached across the table to take Jamie's hand in his. "Why don't you tell us what happened, darling?"

Jamie, feeling utterly exhausted, closed her eyes and swayed from side to side. She was running on fresh air and emotion, and feeling spacey. She needed sleep, but every time she closed her eyes, she saw the devastation in Rowan's eyes and knew she'd put it there. She was the last in a long line of people who'd let him down, and she hated herself for that. But she'd been scared, trying to protect herself—protect *them*—from future hurt.

"When we hooked up, we told each other that we didn't want a relationship, that we were only ever going to be a short-term fling," Jamie explained, her words coming in fits and starts. "Rowan told me he didn't want a relationship—he wasn't interested in commitment. I told him I felt the same."

"Which you probably did, at the time," Chas said, nodding.

Jamie rubbed her forehead with the tips of her fingers. "We agreed to two dates, and we both knew we were heading back to bed. But on that first date, I found out I was pregnant, and he said he'd stick around until I lost the baby, because that's what I expected to happen. I mean, why wouldn't I miscarry since I'd had so many miscarriages?"

Their spines straightened and their eyes narrowed. "What do you mean, you've had so many miscarriages?"

She had to tell them about Kaden and the argument, her lost babies, knowing that she'd done her family a disservice by not trusting them with her secret. How could she move on until the people who loved her knew the truth? In halting words and with lots of tears, she told Greg and Chas the full story of her and Kaden's struggles with having a baby and their deteriorating marriage. They listened in silence, their jaws occasionally dropping.

"We didn't know any of this, James," Greg whispered, his face pale with shock. "How could you not tell us?"

"She's told us now, babe," Chas told him, his hand squeezing his husband's knee. "She told us when she could."

Jamie sent Chas a grateful look. "Anyway, getting back to Rowan... He said that he'd made me pregnant, that he was going to be there until I lost the baby. He didn't bail."

"No, he didn't," Greg agreed.

"We got along so well, and the sex between us was so amazing! I mean—"

Greg slapped his hands over his ears and trilled, "*La-la-la!* I do not need to know about your sex life, James!"

That brought a tiny smile to Jamie's face. "Anyway, we enjoyed each other, but we knew it would end. It had to. I was prepared for that to happen."

"Then you heard that you are actually pregnant and that the baby is healthy," Greg said, his face soft. "That's a pretty damn wonderful thing, Jamie."

Jamie nodded and linked her hands across her tummy. "It really is."

"So why isn't he with you this morning?" Chas asked.

Jamie sent them an anguished look. "He was so excited, guys. Like I'd handed him the world. I'll never forget the joy on his face..."

"But?"

"But then I told him that we have nothing more than sex and a baby in common," Jamie reluctantly admitted.

"And why did you say such a stupid thing?" Greg demanded, shaking his head.

Yeah, now came the hard part—where she had to dig deep and be accountable. To face herself and her fears. "Because I was scared."

"Of what?"

"Of us being swept away by the moment, the excitement! I knew that I would still love him in six months, six years, sixty years, but I don't know if he feels the same. I lost my other babies and I lost Kaden, but I can't lose Rowan! I'll do anything I can to avoid being hurt like that again!"

"So, in your effort to protect yourself, you hurt Rowan by pushing him away." Greg sat on his haunches in front of her and looked up into her face, his eyes somber.

It was a shock to see her happy-go-lucky brother looking so very serious.

"The thing is, Jamie, you have people around you who love you—Mom, Dad, Gran, Chas and me. Rowan had *you,*" Greg insisted.

"No, we weren't—"

"You can bullshit yourself that it didn't mean anything, but he came alive around you. You softened him, made him open up, allowed him the freedom to explore friendships. When we first met, he was a cold, lonely man, but that's not the man he is around you. He's affectionate, funny, caring and honorable. And he thinks the sun rises and sets with you."

She didn't want to hear his words—couldn't. "You don't understand…"

"No, *you* don't understand," Chas said. "Jamie, he loves you. Any fool can see that. Greg and I have this idea that there aren't many people he trusts, even less he's prepared to open up to, but you made him take that chance. Deep down inside, that lost and lonely man wants a partner and a family, somewhere to belong—and he found that with you."

She stared at them, wanting to bat their words away, make them disappear. But they just hung there, refusing to budge. Truth tended to do that.

Jamie wrapped her arms around her stomach and rocked forward, then back. "Oh, God, what have I done?"

"Screwed up," Greg bluntly told her. "And you've probably broken his heart."

Her brother had never been one to pull punches, but it was a fair observation.

"James, we can't protect ourselves against love.

If we do, we dilute it, make it less than. We have to embrace it and trust the idea that it's better to have loved and lost than not loved at all," Chas told her. "You don't regret loving Kaden, do you?"

"No... I...crap."

"But I've been living with soul-eating guilt for more than five years, Greg. Guilt has been my faithful friend."

I have been, it has been...

She was talking in the past tense. Her guilt had, she realized, dissipated, loosened its cold grip on her heart. And—this was harder to admit—maybe part of her pushing Rowan away was her not wanting to let go of her guilt. But she'd paid her penance and maybe it was time to set herself free.

"Rowan helped me realize that Kaden's death was an accident, that we made mistakes, but it wasn't my fault he died," she said, her voice so low it was almost as if she was talking to herself.

"Of course it wasn't!" Greg told her, protective as always.

Chas's next question was accompanied by a soft smile. "So no regrets about Kaden, then? Can you let him go?"

Jamie nodded her head. "Yes, I think I can. I regret the place we were in when he died, but no, I don't regret loving him. I still do."

"And you always will," Chas told her. "But there's a good, honorable and smoking-hot man who wants you in his life. What are you going to do about that?"

"Get him back?" Jamie asked timidly. It was easy to say, hard to do. What if he didn't want to talk to her? What if he'd written her out of his life for good?

Greg stood up, looked at Chas and smiled. "Our work here is done."

Jamie followed him to her feet. "I need to go over to his place, try and talk to him. Where are my car keys, my phone?"

She didn't see the horrified looks Greg and Chas exchanged. "No, baby girl," Chas told her, taking her shoulders and giving her a quick shake. "You need to give him some time to cool off. And you need to sleep. Then you are going to shower, brush your teeth, wash your hair. Because, right now, you look like hell."

She couldn't be that bad. When she protested, Greg walked her over to the mirror in the hallway, and Jamie gasped at her puffy raccoon eyes and blotchy, green-tinged skin. "Ugh."

Greg pulled a face. "Quite."

When Jamie started to climb up the stairs, Greg's comment to Chas drifted up to her. "Seriously, babe, babysitting the kid is going to be super-easy after looking after her. She's exhausting."

"I heard that!" Jamie shouted, not looking back.

"You were supposed to," Chas replied cheekily.

Brothers: 1, Jamie: 0.

Fourteen

In his office, Rowan heard the buzz of his phone and looked down, cursing when he saw Greg's name and number flashing on his screen. He considered dodging the call, but this was Greg's fourth attempt, and Rowan couldn't keep avoiding him forever.

The man was not only Jamie's brother but also his architect. Now he knew, firsthand, why it was never a good idea to work with family.

Rowan answered the call, put Greg on speakerphone and leaned back in his chair. He'd had a raging headache since leaving Jamie's house last night and, although he'd been popping acetaminophen like sweets, the pain hadn't shifted. A couple of times throughout the day, he wondered whether it was his heart that was hurting and not his head.

Then he dismissed that thought as overemotional garbage and went back to work. Or tried to work. So far today, he'd accomplished less than nothing.

"Row, are you there?" Greg asked.

Hearing Jamie's nickname for him from Greg felt like a stake through his heart. "You can call me Rowan or Cowper. Don't shorten my name!"

"Stop being a dick, Rowan," Greg replied, his tone mild. Rowan felt instantly chastised. And embarrassed.

"Sorry," he muttered. "I'm in a shit mood."

"That's not surprising, since my sister is being an idiot," Greg replied. "Are you okay?"

Nobody had ever, ever called him up to check on his emotional state, to ask how he was doing, and Greg's kindness made his eyes burn. *Was* he okay? No. But he would be. Maybe in ten months or in ten years. Who the hell know?

He wanted to lie, to tell Greg that he was perfectly fine, but couldn't force his tongue to form the words. "I will be, I guess. In a hundred years or so."

"Sooner than that, I wager." Before he could ask Greg what he meant by that cryptic statement, Greg spoke again. "Congrats on the baby, by the way. You're going to be a great dad, Rowan."

"How do you know that?" Rowan asked, his voice rough with emotion. "Jesus, Greg, the way I grew up, I wouldn't know what a good dad looked like if it bit me on the ass."

He heard Greg's long sigh. "Rowan, you're a

good person, an honorable man. That's all you need to be a good dad. You'll be okay. I promise."

Rowan didn't think so. Yeah, sure, he'd get to meet his son or daughter in six months or so, but Jamie's absence would be a huge hole he'd never be able to be fill. But, damn, his kid was going to be a lucky little soul, having her as his mother, with excellent grandparents, a great-grandmother and two awesome uncles.

God, he missed Jamie.

In Nashville, whenever he'd started longing for her, he told himself that in a couple of days, he'd be back at her side, back in her bed. That life would be back to normal soon. But last night had been hell on steroids. He'd paced his large apartment, hating the white walls and the white furniture, feeling like he was locked up in an unpadded cell.

He'd woken up, alone in his bed, and decided that he hated his apartment. He didn't think he could spend another minute in it. His opinion hadn't changed. Tonight he'd either sleep on the couch in his office or book a hotel room. He wasn't going to spend another sleepless night in a pseudo-snowstorm.

"Rowan, are you still there?"

Rowan pulled himself back to the present and gripped the bridge of his nose with his thumb and index finger, trying to squeeze the pain away. He needed to distract himself, and that called for a change of subject.

"We need to meet. I have reams of notes about

the design for the eco-development," Rowan told Greg. Then he hesitated, wondering if Greg still intended to work with him. "If you want to back out, now is the time."

Greg took a moment to reply. "I'm gonna pretend you didn't say that, Cowper. And, yeah, let's meet later this week. Why don't you come to our place? We can work and then eat."

He made a face. "I don't know if—"

"Oh, get over yourself, dude," Greg told him. "Jamie is our sister, but you're our friend too. And since you're our niece or nephew's dad, you're now family. I'll text you. Do not wuss out, or I will track you down."

On that threat, Greg disconnected, and Rowan leaned back in his chair once more, shaking his head. Greg and Chas were good people, and he was glad that they weren't choosing sides, that there was space for him in their lives.

He'd made a connection, not only to Jamie but also to her brother and his husband. He hadn't spent much time with her family, but he knew that, had things been different, they could've become his family too.

How could so much have changed in so short a time? What was it about her that just made sense? It was like she'd pushed her hand into his rib cage, grabbed his heart and wouldn't let go. She was beautiful, sure, but he'd known more attractive women. She wasn't perfect. She was stubborn and was as emotionally reserved as he was.

Independent—fiercely so.

But he didn't want perfection. He knew the world was messy. Life had its ups and downs. He wanted a woman who'd had her share of bumps and scrapes, someone who was resilient. He needed a woman in his life who didn't throw up her hands at the first obstacle.

He understood that hearing the baby was viable was a huge shock, an out-of-the-blue thunderbolt, but she hadn't given him a chance to be part of *her* life. Maybe now that she had the baby she so desperately wanted, she didn't need him. She was financially independent, not scared to make her own decisions and she had an excellent support system. What did she need from him? Sex?

She could buy a toy if she wanted to get off.

Screw that. He knew that no machine would come close to matching how he made Jamie feel in bed. He made her squirm and scream, took her to heights he knew were previously unexplored. He got her—in bed and out.

Sure, he wasn't outgoing and couldn't work a crowd like her ex did. He worked too hard, was too ambitious and could only tolerate a few hours at the society events her family attended on a routine basis. But she had a hold on his heart, and he loved her, dammit. He'd never felt this strongly about anyone before—ever—and he knew that, for as long as he lived, she would be the one he wanted to be with. It was that simple...

And that complicated.

He wasn't the type of guy to sit on his ass and accept what was handed to him. He made his luck, and he never admitted defeat. He'd fought for everything he had, established a multimillion dollar business against all the odds.

Jamie wanted to push him away? Well, he could push back too. He could bring his drive and determination to winning her love.

Rowan rubbed his face, feeling edgy and more than a little desperate. He knew what he had to do.

But he didn't have the smallest clue on *how* to accomplish his goal.

After Greg and Chas had ushered her up the staircase, Jamie, beyond exhausted, pulled her drapes closed and climbed back into bed. There was no way she'd sleep. Yet the moment her head hit her pillow, she drifted off and woke up eight hours later, feeling physically refreshed.

Her mind, unfortunately, was still a mess.

After checking the ultrasound photograph— yes, she was pregnant; it hadn't been a dream— she climbed into the shower and washed her hair, trying to process the events of the last twenty-four hours.

She was *pregnant*. The baby intended to stick around, and she was going to be a mom.

She was going to be a *mom*.

No, she was *already* a mom. She was carrying a baby, holding life.

Would her baby have her brown eyes or Rowan's

blue? Her hair or his? Somehow, despite using protection and being careful, she and that amazing man had made a baby.

Their little person, determined as hell, had fought to be here. Jamie smiled. She already knew she had a warrior on her hands. And that was okay; she wanted a kid who challenged her and the status quo, a child who would make her a better mother, a better person.

Her child would be like Rowan in that way.

Rowan challenged her, made her better. He encouraged her to step outside her comfort zone; to live a fuller, more interesting life. He'd helped her come to terms with Kaden's death, and she was slowly trying to forgive herself for arguing with him that dreadful day.

Rowan had given her the one thing she thought she'd never have—a child to hold, guide and raise.

But she didn't want to do it on her own or co-parent at a distance. She wanted to wake up with Rowan, talk to him, spend the night making love.

She wanted him to know that she admired the hell out of him for pulling himself out of what had been an incredibly tough childhood to become a successful businessman, using his intelligence and wits.

After Jamie pulled on a pair of beige capri pants and a white T-shirt, she closed her eyes, cursing herself for her knee-jerk reaction yesterday. Love and good, honorable men didn't come along often. What was wrong with her? Instead of talking through the situation and her feelings, instead of trying to find a way forward, she'd made a unilateral decision for both of them, something she wouldn't have accepted if the shoe was on the other foot.

And it was even worse because Rowan had experienced a series of rejections in the past, and she'd added one more to the list.

She couldn't be more ashamed of herself if she tried.

Jamie couldn't look herself in the eye, so she turned away from the mirror and slipped her feet into a pair of sandals. Not only had she rejected him but she'd also spoiled his I'm-going-to-be-a-daddy moment.

Jamie felt overwhelming remorse and regret. She'd ruined a precious memory for him and had cheated him of feeling excited because she'd wanted to control the situation, because she'd been trying to protect herself.

She didn't know if their relationship could be salvaged, if there was any chance of finding their way back to each other. But she could, maybe, make up for yesterday.

She needed him to know she was sorry, and that she loved him. Loved him fully, utterly, with no qualifications.

He owned her heart. It was time he took charge of it.

Rowan knew he should eat, but he couldn't bear the thought. He was dog-tired, but knew he wouldn't sleep. His concentration was shot, so working wasn't an option. He glanced at his watch and saw that it was nearly half past five. He could go for a run. Maybe exercise would blow the cobwebs away.

He looked up when his PA knocked on his door, carrying a brown box and her bag over her shoulder.

She held up the brown box and walked into his office to place it on his desk. "Oh, this just arrived for you," Belle told him. "'Night."

Rowan stared at the plain box, his attention caught by the lack of shipping labels. The box didn't have his name on it, either, and that was weird. Leaning forward, he reached for it, pulled it to him and slowly lifted the lid.

The box was filled with blue and pink tissue paper, and he cocked his head to the side, intrigued. He couldn't remember when he'd last rustled through paper to find a gift. He carefully lifted each piece, folding it before tackling the next sheet. After folding four sheets, he looked into the box to see a tiny white pile of fabric, folded. He picked it up and lifted it to eye level and saw that it was a tiny onesie. He looked at the label—it was for a newborn baby. His heart jumped into his throat. He'd never realized babies could be that small.

Jamie must've sent this, but why? He turned it around, saw the black writing on what he now realized was the front of the onesie...

Hi Daddy,
Mommy told me you are awesome, and that
you are going to be the best dad ever. I can't
wait to meet you!

Rowan felt his eyes burning and his hands shaking, and he bit his bottom lip. There was something else in the box… He lifted out a simple wooden frame and immediately recognized Jamie's positive pregnancy test affixed to the backing underneath the words "You're Promoted!"

He stared down at the box, not sure what it meant, what he was supposed to do. Call her up and thank her? Hotfoot it over to her house, take her in his arms and kiss her until she couldn't breathe? Option number one was sensible, but option two was his favorite.

He tossed his gifts back into the box, pushed on the lid and reached for his phone and car keys. It would take fifteen minutes to reach her house. God, he hoped she was there. If not, he'd head over to Greg's house, then her parents…

"Going somewhere?"

He whirled around at the sound of her voice, and his knees buckled when he saw her standing in the doorway to his office, her shoulder resting against his doorframe. To a stranger, she'd look relaxed and cool, but he could see that her hands were shaking and immediately noticed the apprehension in her eyes.

"You're here," he stated.

She nodded. "Hey."

He waved her inside and tossed his keys and phone down next to the box. Not knowing what to do with his hands—he wanted to reach for her but couldn't—he jammed them into his pants pockets. They stared at each other, and Rowan wished she'd say something, but when she didn't, he nodded at the box. "Thanks. I...um..."

God, how could he explain how touched he was? How a brown box containing two simple gifts filled him with warmth and gratitude? "You didn't have to," he added gruffly.

She sat down in his visitor's chair and perched on the edge. "I really did. I spoiled what should've been a happy announcement. You deserved better than that, and I'm so sorry."

He leaned his butt against his desk, facing her. "Did you mean it? The words on that baby's garment?"

Her lips twitched. "The onesie? Yeah, I meant it. I've never been so sure of anything in my life."

He pushed his hand through his hair, feeling like he had a golf ball stuck in his throat. "I don't know what to say..."

"Tell me you forgive me for being too much of a coward to tell you yesterday how I feel about you."

Jamie held her breath, watching the emotions fly across his face. For the first time, all his shields were down. She could see his confusion, his shock and the tiny flicker of hope.

"Thank you for our baby, Rowan."

"*Our* baby?" he croaked.

She nodded, suddenly feeling powerful and determined. He was her man. This was their baby and she wasn't leaving here without a) an understanding and b) him.

They were going to be together, raise this child and their other children together, in the same house, sharing their lives. She didn't care if they married or not, but they would be a team, sharing the good and the bad, the ups and the downs of a messy and imperfect life.

"I'm not sure what you want from me, James," Rowan said, his eyes not leaving hers. "I need you to spell it out, in plain language."

Okay, then. She crossed one leg over the other and linked her shaking fingers over her knee. "I am completely, utterly in love with you. I never wanted to be. I fought it, and I am still bone-deep petrified of loving you this much and losing you. But I'd rather be scared and living with you than not having you in my life at all."

He stared at her, his mouth slack with shock. Oh, God, had she gone too far? Had she scared him rigid? Was she asking too much?

She bit her lip before backtracking. "I know it's a lot to take in. And I know you're leery of commitment or being in a relationship, but we *have* been in a relationship these past two months, Row, whether we want to acknowledge it or not. We like each other. We get along well, and the sex is freakin' amazing. If you need some time to get used to the idea—"

"Shut up, James."

She jerked at his low command, confused by the harsh note in his voice.

"You love me?" he asked, his eyes laser-sharp.

She nodded.

He folded his arms, tipped his head to the side and the corners of his mouth lifted. "Okay, then."

Okay, then? What the hell did that mean? She waited for him to continue speaking, and when he didn't, she asked, "That's it? I spill my guts to you and that's your response?"

He slowly shook his head. "No, this is…"

Before she could form another thought, Jamie found herself in his arms, her breasts pushing into his chest, his mouth over hers and his tongue sliding past her teeth. God, she didn't think a man could move so fast or that she could be turned on so quickly. One kiss and she was pulling his shirt out of the waistband of his pants; her hands were on his skin and she was standing on her tiptoes, her mouth fused with his. Rowan groaned, picked her up, and she wound her legs around his hips, rocking against his shaft.

God, she wanted him. Here, now…

Immediately.

Carrying her across the room, Rowan slammed his office door shut, locked it and hit a button next to the door, turning the glass windows dark. Dropping her to her feet, he undid the button to her pants, pushed the fabric down her hips and slid his hand between her legs, causing her to whimper with delight. She opened his belt, undid his pants and pushed her hand inside his underwear, needing to feel him rock-hard in her hand.

When she pulled him free, Rowan picked her up again, rested her back against his office door and pushed inside her, filling her in one sure, hot stroke. Jamie dropped her head back against the door and panted, chasing that sexual high only he could give her.

This wasn't pretty sex, she decided. It was bumpy and fast and hot and sweaty, but it was real and it was theirs—their moment, their life. And when they came together, furious and fast, she knew it was a new start, the birth of a new life.

Minutes later, Rowan rested his head against her forehead and closed his eyes. "Holy crap, sweetheart. That was…intense."

She ran a hand through his hair, held his strong neck in her hand. "If that's going to be your response every time I tell you how I feel, I'll do it all the time."

She couldn't help remembering that she still didn't know how he felt about her. But she wouldn't demand to know. Love not freely given wasn't love at all. She touched his cheek, reached up to gently kiss his mouth. "Are we good?" she asked.

"So good, sweetheart," he told her, resting his cheek against hers. He allowed her to slide down his body and cuddled her close. "No, we are amazing. Let's get cleaned up and then make some plans," he suggested, his big hand stroking her back.

Plans? That sounded like progress.

Dressed again, Rowan handed Jamie a bottle of water and led her over to his leather couch. He pushed her down into the plush cushions before dragging the coffee table sideways and sitting down on it, facing her. He pulled her water bottle out of her grasp, cracked it open and handed it back to her before opening his own bottle and downing half the liquid in one long swallow.

She sipped, her mouth suddenly closing. He looked so serious, like he had a lot on his mind and didn't know where to start. She got it: this was a big deal for him, and she shouldn't rush him. But she was dying here!

"I—"

Rowan shook his head. "My turn to talk."

She wanted to yell at him to start doing just that, but she gathered the little patience she had and tucked her now-bare feet up under her butt.

"I love you, you know. So much."

She looked at him—saw the emotion in his eyes, on his face—and placed her hand on her heart. Such a simple statement but so powerful. And it was all she needed. Just knowing that he loved her meant that nothing was insurmountable. They were a team. Each a half of a whole.

"I'm glad," she replied, just as simply.

He put his water bottle on the coffee table next to him and leaned his forearms on his knees, his eyes on hers. "I didn't want to love you, and I thought I could resist you. I thought I wanted a solitary, shallow life, but you changed all that."

"By getting pregnant?"

He shook his head. "No. I would've fallen for you baby or no baby—I probably was in love with you from the moment we met. I think you are what I need, the one person I was looking for."

Jamie sighed, overcome by a rush of emotion. His love wasn't linked to her carrying his child. That was such a relief because their love was based on who they were to each other.

"I'm so happy to hear that," Jamie told him. "I've been living in a vacuum since Kaden died, but you brought me back, Row. I don't think anyone but you could've done that."

He leaned forward and kissed her softly, gently—an I-can't-wait-for-what-comes-next kiss.

Pulling back, he nodded at the box still sitting on his desk. "Why did you send me those things?"

She smiled. "I felt bad because I spoiled the moment. I told you I was pregnant and immediately insisted you shouldn't get excited because I'd lose the baby. Then, when I found out our baby was healthy, I spoiled that moment too. I hoped the small gifts made up for that, just a little."

He shook his head. "They aren't small to me. Did you mean it?"

She knew exactly what he was asking: Did she

218 CROSSING TWO LITTLE LINES

mean what was written on the onesie? "Absolutely. You're such a good man, Rowan. I'm proud of what you've done with your life, how you've battled the odds and won. I intend to make damn sure that our kids know how awesome their dad is."

"'Kids'?" Rowan asked, cocking his head. "More than one?"

She grinned. "Oh, hell yes." She tapped her stomach. "This little person is going to need company. Are you okay with that?"

He looked a little bemused and shell-shocked, but he nodded. "Yeah."

She patted his knee, laughing at the hint of fear she saw in his eyes. "After two, we'll consider another. Deal?"

He smiled. "Deal. But only if you marry me."

It was her turn to feel blindsided. "Marriage?" she squeaked. "Seriously?"

"Mmm," he murmured, his eyes full of laughter.

"But you don't *want* to get married."

"I want to marry *you*. I want to call you my wife, be your husband, do this properly."

Well, all right, then. She released her breath and tried to get the world to stop spinning. At best, she'd hoped that Rowan would move in.

"There are benefits to getting married that you haven't thought about," Rowan told her, linking his fingers in hers. "Your mother will never worry about your love life again."

"True enough. But marrying me means taking

on my family, Row. I love them and they are a big part of my life."

"I like your family, and I'm already good friends with Greg and Chas. Greg called me yesterday to check up on me. I appreciate that. Luckily, I can afford to let your grandmother fleece me at poker, and your dad can teach me golf." He looked down, scratched his forehead. "I need a family, James. I need you and the family we'll create."

He was right—he did. And she needed him. To love her, to cherish her, to be her lover and her friend, her partner as they tried to win at life.

"Well?" Rowan asked her, the small smile on his face suggesting he already knew her answer. "Will you be my first and last love?"

Her heart sighed, then sighed again as joy slid through her veins. "Absolutely. In this lifetime. And the next."

* * * * *

If you liked this book, don't miss
Dynasties: DNA Dilemma
from Joss Wood!
Available now.

Secrets of a Bad Reputation
Wrong Brother, Right Kiss
Lost and Found Heir
The Secret Heir Returns

#2893 VACATION CRUSH
Texas Cattleman's Club: Ranchers and Rivals
by Yahrah St. John
What do you do after confessing a crush on an accidental livestream? Take a vacation to escape the gossip! But when Natalie Hastings gets to the resort, her crush—handsome rancher Jonathan Lattimore—is there too. Will one little vacation fling be enough?

#2894 THE MARRIAGE MANDATE
Dynasties: Tech Tycoons • by Shannon McKenna
Pressured into marrying, heiress Maddie Moss chooses the last man in the world her family will accept—her brother's ex–business partner, Jack Daly. Accused of destroying the company, Jack can use the opportunity to finally prove his innocence—but only if he can resist Maddie...

#2895 A RANCHER'S REWARD
Heirs of Hardwell Ranch • by J. Margot Critch
To earn a large inheritance, playboy rancher Garrett Hardwell needs a fake fiancée—fast! Wedding planner Willa Statler is the best choice. The problem? She's his best friend's younger sister! With so much at stake, will their very real connection ruin everything?

#2896 SECOND CHANCE VOWS
Angel's Share • by Jules Bennett
Despite their undeniable chemistry, Camden Preston and Delilah Hawthorn are separating. With divorce looming, Delilah is shocked when her blind date at a masquerade gala turns out to be her husband! The attraction's still there, but can they overcome what tore them apart?

#2897 BLACK SHEEP BARGAIN
Billionaires of Boston • by Naima Simone
Abandoned at birth, CEO Nico Morgan will upend the one thing his father loved most—his company. Integral to the plan is a charming partner, and that's his ex, Athena Evans. But old feelings and hot passion could derail everything...

#2898 SECRET LIVED AFTER HOURS
The Kane Heirs • by Cynthia St. Aubin
Finding his father's assistant at an underground fight club, playboy Mason Kane realizes he isn't the only one leading a double life. So he offers Charlotte Westbrook a whirlwind Riviera fling to help her loosen up, but it could cost her job and her heart...

SPECIAL EXCERPT FROM

(H) HARLEQUIN
DESIRE

*Home due to tragedy, exes Felicity Vance and
Wynn Oliver don't expect to see one another, but Wynn
needs a caregiver for the baby niece now entrusted in
his care. But when one hot night changes everything,
will secrets from their past ruin it all?*

Read on for a sneak peek at
The Comeback Heir
by USA TODAY *bestselling author Janice Maynard*

"This won't work. You know it won't." Felicity
continued. "If the baby is your priority, then you and
I can't…"

Can't what?" Wynn smiled mockingly.

"You're taunting me, but I don't know why."

"You don't want to *enjoy* each other while you're
here?"

"We had our chance. We didn't make it work. And
I'm not one for fooling around just for a few orgasms."

"The old Fliss never said things like that."

"The old *Felicity* was an eighteen-year-old kid."

"You always seemed mature for your age. You had
a vision for your future and you made it happen. I'm
proud of you."

HDEXP0722R

She gaped at him. "Thank you."

"I'm sorry," he said gruffly. "I shouldn't have kissed you. Let's pretend it never happened. A fresh start, Fliss. Please?"

"Of course. We're both here to honor Shandy and care for her daughter. I don't think we should do anything to mess that up."

"Agreed."

Don't miss what happens next in...
The Comeback Heir
by USA TODAY *bestselling author Janice Maynard.*

Available September 2022 wherever
Harlequin Desire books and ebooks are sold.

Harlequin.com